WALK
IN MY SHOES

HEARTWARMING AND
INSPIRATIONAL
SHORT STORIES

JIM
SURMANEK

**outskirts
press**

For my kids and grandkids:
Keri, Kim, Dan, Emily, Zach,
Cassie, Logan, and Riley

Contents

L arry took a swig of his beer and said, "The guy's good."
"I agree. I wouldn't be surprised if the big guys grab him pretty damn quick." Gabe put up his hand, signaling Larry to stop talking. With a low, almost whisper voice, Gabe said, "Here it comes." One second later Gabe screamed out, "Yes!"

Larry got up so fast from his seat that he almost fell on top of the guy sitting in front of him. His hotdog went flying in the air, but he paid no mind to it. Nor did the guy that it landed on. The fans went crazy with cheers and gyrations. Gabe said, "Bliss just pitched a no-hitter! Geez, he's good!"

After all the back-smacking and high-fives were finished, the coach pulled Bliss aside. "You didn't know it, Gary, but Henry Rotkin was in the stands. He wants to have a word with you after you get into your civvies."

"Rotkin's Triple-A, isn't he?"

"Yup. It's good news for you and bad news for me. If you move up, make that *when* you move up, I'll be losing the best pitcher the Wildcats ever had."

Gary smiled the biggest smile he ever had. "Thanks, Coach. I owe you a lot for all you've done for me."

"Bull, Gary. You did it, not me."

As a minor leaguer Gary had to deal with a near

poverty-level of income playing for the Wildcats farm team. He had to work extra jobs to afford to live – all while trying to accomplish his dream of playing in the majors. If Rotkin was going to move him to Triple-A, his dream might soon become a reality.

———=((◐))=———

Jennie pulled her car up to the donation area at Goodwill and was greeted by Christopher. "Hi there. Making a donation today?"

"Yes, and I could use your help." She and Christopher unloaded several boxes and a large assortment of men's clothing – some on hangers, some neatly folded.

It was apparent that the amount of clothing indicated a man no longer needed everything that was in his closet. Jennie was a beautiful woman. Long black hair accentuated her dark eyes. He knew she was 24-years-old and that her husband was no longer with her. Always wanting to help people in need, Christopher quietly asked Jennie, "Have you suffered a loss?"

Jennie paused before answering. She swallowed, took a breath, and said, "Yes. My husband was killed a couple of years ago. In Afghanistan. He was a soldier."

"My deepest sympathy. I'm Christopher. If there is anything I can do for you, besides taking your donations, please let me. Please. It fills my heart when I can help people."

"Thank you, Christopher. That's very nice of you. But I'll be okay."

"This seems petty and I apologize, but we're supposed to ask if you want a receipt for tax purposes."

Jennie smiled. "No need. I just hope whoever buys any of my husband's...." She didn't complete the sentence. She started to cry. Wiping her tears, she regained her composure and said, "I'm sorry."

Christopher gently put his hand on her shoulder. "I understand." She stood there, looking at Christopher. His kind face and gentle touch comforted her. He knew she wanted to say something to him, perhaps something about her husband, but he knew better than to press her. "Would you like to sit for a moment? I have a spare bottle of water if you'd like to have it."

Jennie took another deep breath and smiled with a half-smile. "You're very kind, but I should be going. Goodbye."

"Goodbye." He unpacked the first box and saw a pair of cowboy boots. They looked brand new, but he knew Jennie's husband had worn them a few times. He took a cleaning rag and wiped the little bit of dust that accumulated on them, and set them aside so he could put them on display in the men's shoe rack. He thought, *you're going to get around, boots.*

———◅◦(◉)◦▻———

Gary looked at the young woman as she approached. He was immediately attracted to her very pretty face and dark eyes, surrounded by long black hair. He knew better than to flirt while he was on his job at the Brew for You Coffee Bar, so he smiled and said, "Welcome. What can we make for you today?"

"I'll have the mocha frap, the middle size one."

"You got it. May I have your name?"

"Just my name? Not my number?"

Gary was accustomed to hearing lines like that. It wasn't because he was a baseball player – not many people follow farm team games and players. He just happened to be what many young women would call a stud. He believed in a *relationship* when it came to having sex, not one-night stands, although his libido sometimes went into over-drive. "Well, we're not allowed to take numbers, so just your name."

"Colleen. My last name is 322 440 1877."

"Thanks. We'll get going on that drink right now."

The day continued like just about all other days. His salary, plus tips, gave him a reasonable chunk of change to add to the paltry salary he received as a baseball player, but he still had to be frugal so he could afford necessities and a beer with his buddies now and then.

His morning shift ended at eleven o'clock. Practice was scheduled at Warton Field for three o'clock. which left plenty of time to have lunch and relax. Enroute to the field on his inexpensive and old 60cc bike, he stopped at In-N-Out for a #1 combo – not expensive, but filling. Across the street was a Goodwill store. He looked down at his unpolished and marred shoes. As comfortable as they were, he didn't think they made the right statement about him. He decided to drop in the store to see if he could get another pair. Cheap, of course.

While at the display of men's shoes, he heard a scream. He looked around to see who was screaming, and saw a guy at check-out and a cashier who was nervously opening the register. Christopher called out to the cashier, "Everything okay, Isabel?" Her face was filled with fear as she nodded 'no' with the least amount of movement. As he walked towards her, Christopher called out, "Young man. Can I help you?"

The man brandished a knife and pointed it at Christopher. "Get the hell away old man." Christopher stopped. He wasn't in fear for his life. He knew he couldn't die. He was concerned that agitating the robber might cause Isabel to be hurt.

Gary witnessed the scene – the cashier's fear, the Goodwill employee's advances, and the robber with the knife. He wanted to help. From his position in the store the robber couldn't see him. Gary thought to rush him, dive at him and knock him down, but quickly realized it was a fool's tactic. He grabbed a cowboy boot off the rack and hurled it at the robber at a speed that matched his 95-mph fastball. It was a *strike*, a strike to the head. The boot's heel hit the robber in his temple. Down he went.

Goodwill employees rushed to the scene. One of them used his belt to tie the robber's hands behind his back. Another grabbed a necktie from the rack and tied the robber's ankles. Another called 911. Isabel was still panicked. She stood at her register, crying and shaking, still holding the register's money in her hand. Christopher also came on the scene. He held his hands on her shoulders. "Isabel, it's over. You're safe."

Gary went to the check-out. As if he again pitched a no-hitter, the employees patted him on his back, cheering him for stopping the robbery. Typically modest about his accomplishments, Gary said, "Would you like me to put the boot back?" Everyone laughed.

"You're a hero, young man. You saved the day," said Christopher.

Isabel calmed. She went to Gary and kissed him on the cheek. "Christopher's right. You are a hero. Thank you, thank you, thank you."

With a smile and jovial tone, Christopher said, "No, you don't need to put the boot back. I'm sure the police will want to talk to you, so you better stick around for a while." Gary looked at his watch. He still had time to wait and still make practice on time.

Six minutes later two cops entered Goodwill. Gary asked if he could be questioned first because he had to get to Wharton Field by three o'clock. The cops obliged him. They jotted down the information from his driver's license, questioned him about the incident, and told him they'd be in touch if they needed anything else. "Thank you, Mr. Bliss. You're one of the good guys." As he walked out, Christopher handed him a shopping bag. In it were the boots – shiny, unmarred alligator boots. "I think you should have these, Mr. Bliss. You can mount them in your trophy case with all of the baseball trophies you're going to win."

"How'd you know I play baseball?"

Christopher didn't give one hint in word or gesture how he really knew, and said, "Only a baseball player can throw a boot like you did."

———— ◉ ————

Meg, a petit young woman wearing very large eyeglasses and a baseball cap bearing the Wildcat's insignia, walked up to Gary. It was Friday, the day after the Goodwill incident. He gave her the usual greeting: "Hi. Great hat! What can we get for you today?"

"A story. People need to hear a good story about a good guy."

"Hmm. Do you want a small, medium, or large story? Hot or iced?"

"Very funny." She held up her smart phone and asked, "Is this you? Are you Gary Bliss?"

Gary looked at the photo on the phone. It was from his driver's license. He thought *How the hell did she get that photo? Is she a cop?* "Ha! I didn't know my photo was on Facebook."

"When's your next break so we can sit and talk for a bit?"

"Twenty minutes."

"I'll be sitting at that corner table drinking a small green tea. Hot." There was an awkward silence. "Mr. Bliss, I'd like to order a green tea."

"Ah, sure. Green tea. Small. Hot. We'll get right on it."

Twenty minutes later Gary joined Meg at the corner table. "So, miss, who are you and what do you want? Why do you have my driver's license photo?"

"I'm a reporter for Fox News. I do a segment called *Feel Good Stories*. It's human-interest stuff. Viewers love it. You, Mr. Bliss, did something that I know people will want to know about."

"The no-hitter was last week. It's really not a big deal."

"Goodwill, Mr. Bliss. The cowboy boot? The robber?"

"Yeah, I remember that."

"My boyfriend was one of the cops that came to the scene. I had to really twist his arm to get your information." She raised her hands in the air and acted like a magician. "Ta dah!"

"Is he out of the hospital?"

"My boyfriend? He wasn't in the hospital."

"Well, I just thought, with a twisted arm and all."

"Very funny. But seriously, I would like to hear about the robbery."

Meg asked many questions and Gary gave many answers. She took his photo with her smart phone – better, she thought, to air a current photo of a good-looking guy than the five-year-old photo of him when he got his license.

The story aired that night. It was entitled *Booted Out of Goodwill*.

⸻◉⸻

Two days after Gary was featured on *Feel Good Stories,* he came out of the locker room at Wharton Field. He noticed the crowd was larger, a lot larger than usual. He walked onto the field and heard the fans yelling in unison. "Boots! Boots! Boots!" His coach came up to him and said, "I guess we'll have to take Bliss off your jersey and sew on Boots."

Gary was thrilled by the roar of the crowd. He also liked his new nickname. He waved his hat in the air as he went to the pitcher's mound, humbly nodding in thanks.

Gary pitched well. Not a no-hitter, but after nine innings the Wildcats won the game by one run. He was more pleased that the team won than he was that he pitched well. As he walked off the field the fans again screamed out his name. "Boots! Boots! Boots!"

A small crowd awaited him when he left the

stadium, holding pieces of paper, a baseball, or a Wildcats cap. He gladly and graciously autographed the paraphernalia.

Jennie had read the newspaper article about Boots, and wondered if Boots actually used the boots she had donated to Goodwill. When the crowd thinned, Jennie saw Gary wearing them and walked toward him.

He thought he recognized her. "Colleen?"

"No. Jennie. You got those boots at Goodwill, didn't you?"

Gary smiled and said, "Yes. Nice, no?"

"Those are them," she said.

"Those are them, what?"

"Are those the ones you used to stop the robber?"

"Yeah. In fact, they gave them to me as a thank you."

With a very sweet voice, Jennie said, "Thank you Mr. Bliss. Bye."

As she turned away, Gary touched her arm and said, "Wait."

She turned around and faced him. He didn't say anything for a couple of seconds. He just looked at her. She didn't say anything either, and just looked at him. It wasn't an awkward moment. It was a moment both of them had while connecting to each other.

She broke the silence. "I donated those boots to Goodwill. They were my husbands." She paused, bowed her head and looked down. It was clear to Gary that she was emotionally upset. He remained silent. Jennie continued by saying, "He died in combat in Afghanistan. And now Goodwill donated his boots to you. I just find that, well, I find that...interesting."

Gary said, "Jennie, I'm not one to believe in things

like *This was meant to be.* You know, destiny kind of stuff. But what if it was?"

"Meant to be?" she said. Her face glowed. It wasn't the sun shining on her. It wasn't embarrassment. It was the warm feeling that she felt.

"I'm pretty sure we should talk about the boots some more. Want to have coffee with a baseball player?"

Jennie nodded gently, smiled and said, "Yes, we should, and yes I would."

Greyhound

T he dense fog on that Wednesday night made driving difficult. The Greyhound bus, traveling well below the speed limit, stopped. The driver saw a red light flashing in the middle of the two-lane highway. He opened the door when he saw a man approaching the bus. "What's going on?"

The man stepped up into the bus, and swung his sawed-off, pump-action shotgun around from behind his back. Pointing it at the driver, he said, "I'm going on." He reached in front of the driver, yanked out the two-way radio, and stomped on it with his boot. Passengers who were still awake looked out the windows and saw nothing but blackness. Only those in the first few rows saw the man and his gun. Those that were sleeping didn't wake up – not until they heard the noise. Rudy nearly peed his pants when he heard the pump-action shotgun racking and saw the robber standing next to the driver. "No worries, folks. No one is gonna get hurt if you jus' do like I say." Dressed in a black shirt, black pants, black hat, and a Batman-like mask, the robber succeeded in looking ominous.

Rudy was traveling back home from his summer job as a golf caddy in an upstate resort. His job netted him just over $2,000, all of it in $100 bills in his backpack. He slid his backpack well under his seat.

"Now I'm going to ask each one of you to come here. See this bucket on the floor? You're gonna put all your stuff in it. Stuff is wallets, phones, watches, rings, necklaces and things like that." The robber then shot off one of the cartridges, putting a hole in the roof. "Now you mighta thought this isn't a real shotgun. Still thinkin' that?" He racked it again. He screamed out, "Phones! I know all of ya got phones. If ya don't, ya need to get with the times and buy one." He laughed at what he thought was a funny line. "Throw ya phones on the floor so I can see 'em. If I see anyone making a phone call, my little Browning baby here is going to kiss your ass."

He pointed to a lady in the front row, telling her to come forward and drop her stuff in the bucket. Shaking, she rose from her seat, walked a few steps to the bucket, and emptied her purse. "Watch?" She then took off her watch and put that in the bucket. "Do I have to say ring and necklace?" She put both of those in the bucket and then returned to her seat. The robber then pointed to the second passenger in the front, and proceeded through the rows. Rudy was next to be called to the front.

"Get up here, kid." Rudy froze. He was in fear of being shot, but more so that the robber was going to take all of his money. The robber walked several rows up and pointed the shotgun at Rudy's head. "Maybe you don't hear good." The robber then screamed out, "Get your ass up there and put your stuff in it." Rudy slowly got out of his seat and started walking to the front of the bus. "Very funny, kid. Get your ass back here and get that sack under your seat." Rudy had no choice but to comply. He bent down in front of the robber, thinking he would be kicked if he resisted getting his bag. He noticed a skull painted on the robber's boot, which added to his fear.

After all of the twenty passengers put all of their stuff in the robber's bucket, he grabbed it and backed out down the steps. The passengers then heard the shotgun fire. The bus driver yelled out, "Don't worry, folks. He just shot out a tire. Help will be arriving soon."

When the bus didn't arrive at its next scheduled stop, the diner manager called the cops. Soon thereafter the cops arrived at the stranded bus. Everyone testified as to what happened. As if the fog outside crept into their heads, the passengers' memories of what happened were not clear. Descriptions of the robber varied from tall to average, slim to heavy, early 30s to late 50s. Likewise, the shotgun was described as a shotgun, rifle, pistol, and some kind of gun. No one could describe the robber's car, and none saw the license plate.

⊷⊷⊷«◉»⊶⊶⊶

"I understand, son. I'm just happy that you weren't hurt. We'll figure out the money somehow," said Rudy's father. Rudy's mother died a year earlier. She was the primary breadwinner in the family. His father worked hard at the factory, but his pay was barely enough to pay the bills and buy groceries. Rudy decided to quit the football team in the fall, and find a job to help with finances.

"I'll quit football, Dad."

"No, I don't want you to do that. You love the game and the team needs you."

"They'll find another quarterback. I'm not the only guy that can throw a football. And besides, I'll be graduating in a year and somebody will have to take my place anyway."

"Son, I appreciate what you want to do, but..."

Rudy interrupted him. "Good, I'm glad you appreciate what I want to do. And right back at you, Dad."

On Friday morning Rudy decided to scout the town's shops to see if he could get a part-time job where he could work after school let out, and possibly on weekends. The hunt became a collection of *sorrys* and *nos.* The barber shop was willing to hire him for only one hour a day to sweep and clean sinks. The pay was miniscule. None of the restaurants needed a dishwasher. The supermarkets had no openings, nor did the drug stores.

Frustrated, Rudy took a seat on the bench in front of the Ace Hardware store to think about what he should do.

He took a swig of water from the bottle he had in his backpack. When he put the bottle down, he saw a dog sitting in front of him. It was a long, lean, gray dog. Rudy thought it might have been a Greyhound. "You looking for a job too?" The dog didn't answer. "Want some water?" Rudy thought that the dog understood that question when its tongue swerved across its mouth. Rudy poured some water in his hand and offered it to the dog. On the second offering, the dog was startled when it heard the clanking of the door shutting as a woman exited Ace. The sound was similar to the ratcheting noise Rudy remembered hearing on the Greyhound bus.

The dog ran away, past the woman. The woman

was rifling through her purse, and not paying attention to the sidewalk when she was distracted by the dog running past her. She tripped. As a football player Rudy learned to be agile and a quick thinker. When the woman fell forward Rudy sprang from the bench and caught her before she hit the pavement. "Oh my, thank you, thank you."

"Glad to help, ma'am. Glad you weren't hurt."

"No, not at all. Well, my pride, and maybe my shoe." She looked down and saw that the heel of her high heel shoe had broken off. Rudy picked it up and gave it to her. He said, "You might be at the right place. Ace might be able to fix it for you."

"Now that just might be."

Thinking that she might need help walking, he held out his arm so she could hold on to him. She took off her unbroken shoe and proceeded to walk into the store barefooted. "Marty," she called out. "Tom, where's Marty?" Just then Marty came to her from the Screws-Nails-Fasteners aisle.

"Did you forget something, Claire?"

"No, Marty. I came back because this young man embraced me."

Marty said, "What?"

Rudy said, "Huh?"

Claire laughed. "Oh, I just wanted to make a little joke about the incident." She explained to Marty about her fall and the young hero who saved her.

"Thank you, son. What's your name?"

"Rudy."

"Rudy, I'd like to give you a thank you gift for saving the life of my favorite wife."

Claire said, "I know I'm your favorite 'cause I'm the

only one you got." She kissed him on the cheek and then pinched it.

Both of them smiled at each other.

"What would you like, Rudy? I mean, what would you like that is reasonable?"

Rudy did not answer immediately. He looked around the store and saw aisle after aisle of the thousands of items for sale. He saw employees walking around, tidying this or that, and helping customers. He saw cashiers at the cash registers. He saw a man standing in front of a paint-can shaking machine waiting for it to stop. All in all, he saw people working. Rudy responded to Marty, "A job, sir."

―――――――――――――・《◎》・―――――――

Rudy arrived for work at Ace every day, right after school. His part time job was for three hours a day on school days, plus six hours on Saturday. His duties were primarily stocking shelves and keeping them neat and clean. He was often asked by a customer "Where's the...?" and would escort the customer to the right place in an aisle. He liked what he was doing, and he liked Marty and all of the employees. His dad was proud of his commitment, and both of them benefited financially.

After a few weeks on the job, exactly four weeks after the bus robbery, an elderly man came up to him in the Lights-Fixtures-Electrical aisle. "Perhaps you can help me," the man said.

"Sure. What do you need?"

"Do you sell work boots?"

"Sorry to say, we don't. There's a great place down the block, Todd's Shoes, and I think they sell work boots."

Shaking his head in agreement, the customer said, "Yes, I was in there. I just can't afford the prices they charge."

Rudy was hesitant to make his next suggestion, but decided better to offer help with the possibility of an insult, then not help at all. "Ya know, I was at Goodwill the other day to buy some things. A lot of people think Goodwill is for poor people. It isn't. They have great things there, some almost brand new, and the prices are good."

"You're right, son. I'll give them a try." He looked at Rudy's work shirt and pointed at his name. "I'll tell them that Rudy recommended them. By the way, my name is Christopher." Christopher extended his hand and Rudy shook it.

An hour later Rudy was on his knees stocking a bottom shelf with painting supplies. A man approached him, and as he did, Rudy shivered and became tense. He recognized who it was. Not his face, because he never saw his face. The customer was wearing the same boots as the Greyhound robber – black with red laces and a white skull painted on the side of each boot. He didn't think about that when he was questioned by the cops, but his memory of them was vivid. The man said, "Hey, kid."

Rudy was hoping that the man didn't recognize him. He thought about running away, but didn't when a new thought came to mind: *What if he has that shotgun?* He then had a third thought: *The boots don't necessarily mean he's the guy.* Rudy took his chances, got up and said, "How can I help you?"

"Where are the chainsaws?"

"Down this aisle, make a right at the end, and go two aisles up."

Pointing down the aisle, the man said, "That way?" That's when Rudy was convinced that he was the robber. The robber's hand flashed across his mind. He remembered that the robber had a tattoo of a dragon on the back of his left hand – another detail that the trauma blocked from his mind when questioned by the police. "Yes, that way." Without a thank you, the man... the robber...walked away.

Rudy walked quickly to the Garden Tools - Fertilizer aisle, picked out a long-handled spade shovel, and went to Marty to tell him about the man. "He is definitely the Greyhound bus robber!" Excited by the situation, but able to control his emotions, Rudy whispered, "911?"

Just then the robber was seen at the cashier. He paid for the chainsaw with cash, got a receipt, and left the store. The cops hadn't arrived. Rudy followed him out. The man tossed the chainsaw in the bed of his pickup truck, got in and started his engine. Concerned that he would flee before the cops arrived, Rudy went to the front of his truck, and yelled out, "You stole my money!" He swung his shovel at the windshield, shattering it. The robber got out of his truck. Rudy held the shovel as if it was a baseball bat, thinking, I feel a homerun coming. Sweat started to trickle down his face. His sole purpose was to stop the robber, shrugging off any concern about his own safety.

A siren screeched when a police cruiser pulled up. A cop on a bullhorn said, "This is the police. Don't move! Stay where you are!" The man turned and picked-up the chainsaw. He stood there, chainsaw in hand, eyeing Rudy, and disregarding the cops. The cop's demands continued. "Do not move! Put the chainsaw down! Now!" The robber didn't comply. He started to walk towards Rudy. One second later the cop shot the BolaWrap at him. The robber's arms and legs were immediately wrapped by a rope. He couldn't move. The cop spoke out loudly to the crowd of people that gathered to witness the incident. "All done folks. We got this tied-up. No need to worry anymore."

The next day the newspaper headline read:

GREYHOUND ROBBER NABBED

The story recounted the crime, and gave exacting details of how the robber was captured. Rudy was mentioned several times in the article. The Police Chief was quoted as saying, "It's citizens like Rudy that make our community a great place to live." Marty was also quoted, saying, "We hired a great kid and found out he was even greater than we thought."

A principal at his high school went on the P.A. system and said, "Teachers and students, please thank Rudy Clemens the next time you see him. I'm declaring today the official Rudy is a Hero Day."

"I am very proud of you, Rudy. You took charge and did the right thing," said his dad.

Rudy smiled, and brushed off his comment by saying, "Piece of cake, Dad. All in a day's work."

"Talk about a piece of cake, son, that $5,000 reward that Greyhound gave to you is certainly a big piece." They both laughed.

"And the cherry on top, Dad. Don't forget the $500 bonus Marty gave me."

His dad said, "That $500 is totally for you, not for us. Spend it on whatever you want."

————))(((————

Sitting on a lounge chair in Goodwill's donation area, Christopher read the newspaper article. When finished, he smiled, touched the crucifix on his necklace, and got back to work.

A lice knocked and simultaneously opened the door to her brother's house. "Hey, Indy, how are you?" She petted him and screeched out, "Frank! I'm here, you lazy bum!"

Frank wheeled into the front room from his bedroom. "You again. It must be Saturday. I haven't seen you since last Saturday."

"I'm fine, Frank. Thanks for asking."

"Come on, Al. You know I love you. You've always been my favorite sister."

"I'm your only sister, Stupid. Are you getting senile?"

"I don't remember." He laughed, but she didn't.

Indy went to Frank and smelled his feet. "This dog must think I have doggie treats in my socks. Always smelling my feet."

Alice snorted and said, "If you took a bath more than once a week, maybe he wouldn't be smelling you so much."

"Thanks for the compliment."

"Sorry, Frank. I had a bad week and I shouldn't be taking it out on you."

Alice went into the kitchen to make coffee, and Frank wheeled to the worn-out spot on his carpet in front of the TV. He clicked on ESPN to watch the NASCAR racers. Soon thereafter, Alice went into the family room, placed Frank's coffee on the table, and said, "What a surprise. NASCAR."

"Ha, ha," he said. Just because I can't be involved in it anymore doesn't mean I don't like watching it."

Alice said, "I have a surprise for you, my dear bro."

"Do tell."

She reached into her purse, and had a Cheshire Cat grin on her face. "I bought a raffle ticket at the church benefit last Sunday. I won."

"A vacation? A new vacuum cleaner?"

"Nope. I won two tickets to Sunday's NASCAR races at the Elliott Racetrack. "We're going, Frank. Tomorrow. Before you say *no way*, I'm telling you We! Are! Going!"

Frank put his coffee down. Looking sullen, he said, "You're a doll, and I love you. But I can't do that. It'll rip my heart out."

"Frank, you've been beating yourself up for nearly two years now. Okay, fine, you can't be the top mechanic on the McGowan team anymore, but you can watch the race and hoot and holler...get into it...not on the boob tube, but live." She knelt down in front of him, and placed her hands on his knees. Indy went to her side and sat next to her. Frank's dog must have thought they were playing a game and he wanted to be part of it. But it was not a game. It was a plea by Alice for her brother, whom she loved dearly, to be happy. She didn't say any words. She just looked at Frank, letting her eyes tell him what she didn't have words to say.

Frank sat quietly, looking down at his legs. He had no memory of the accident, but did find out what happened. He was on the creeper under Butch McGowan's

Chevrolet SS checking for a fuel leak. He was sliding out from under when the jack stand gave way.

After two days in the hospital, with both legs in traction, and having undergone various medical tests, the surgeon told him the news that would change his life. "I'm sorry to say that we do not recommend surgery on your legs."

Frank asked why, and discovered he had two medical problems that made surgery very risky: Prediabetes and chronic low blood pressure. He could have died while under the knife. He chose life without workable legs to death. Now, almost two years later, he wished he had taken the chance and had the surgery.

Frank heard Alice's plea, and saw it in her eyes. "Does that mean I have to put on clean socks tomorrow?" Alice laughed, and pinched his cheek.

—————◆———

Alice wheeled Frank up the ramp towards the *Handicap Entrance* sign. Frank didn't like the sign, saying to Alice, "Do they have to remind people with a handicap that they're handicapped?"

"Oh, stop it now, Frank. Think about how easy it is to get in, and to have great seats."

"Yeah, right. Great seats. You mean a slab of flat concrete where all of us *handicapped people* can hang out."

"Stop being so cranky. If you keep it up I'm tellin' you, no hot dog, no beer!"

"Well, if you put it that way, I'd love to sit on concrete. Don't forget the mustard and relish."

Once Frank was situated and comfortable, Alice went off to the concession stand. Christopher sat down on the stadium seat next to him. "Sorry, Bud, that seat's for my sister."

"Of course. I'll just take that seat behind you. Sorry."

Alice returned just when the cars were lined up on the track. The announcer boomed, "Gentleman, start your engines!" The thunderous roar of engines combined with the noise from cheering fans was deafening. "Here's your dog and beer," Alice yelled. Frank didn't hear her, not that he wanted to. He didn't take his eyes off the cars. "Frank!" she yelled again. Still no response. Christopher tapped Frank's shoulder causing him to turn his head. He saw Alice holding his dog and beer, smiled, took the beer in one hand and the dog in the other, and just held it. He had zero interest in the food. Alice nodded thank-you to Christopher.

"Green flag, Alice. Here it comes." The starter waved the flag, the cars accelerated, and the race was on. Frank sat holding his beer and dog. He leaned forward now and then, yelling at one or another driver, telling them to *get in the groove!* or *slingshot, kid!* Alice watched Frank as he was mesmerized by the race. He showed an energy, a happiness that Alice hadn't seen for a long, long time. She took his hotdog and beer from him and placed it on the concrete, knowing that Frank would invariably have had an accident with it. She did it just in time. Frank threw his arm up with a fist-pump, and screamed *Yahoo!*

He looked down at the pit-stops, occasionally mumbling and shaking his head. He didn't think one or another of the crew members were doing their job as best they could. He wanted to run to them to tell them how things should be done. He yelled at them, but his words got sucked into the sound of screaming engines.

Nearly three hours later the checkered flag was waved and the race ended. Alice knew four hours had passed; Frank felt like it was an hour. Walking and wheeling back to the parking lot, Frank didn't shut-up about the race. He gave Alice color-commentary about the cars, the drivers, and the pit crew. It was gibberish to Alice, but a beautiful song to Frank.

<hr />

"Thank you, Alice."

"You're welcome, Frank. I thought the steak was a little tough, but I guess it was okay."

He put his knife and fork down, reached out to touch her hand, and said, "I mean about kicking me in the ass and taking me to the race."

"Yeah, it was a good Sunday for you, wasn't it?"

Indy barked when he heard the knock on the front door. Alice opened the door. "Can I help you?" she asked. She recognized the man from the racetrack. "Wait - weren't you at the racetrack earlier? And now that I think about it, weren't you at church last Sunday?"

Frank saw Christopher standing there and said, "We don't want to know about Jehovah."

Christopher avoided answering Alice's questions. "My name's Christopher." He held-up a wallet, and said, "I'm not a Jehovah Witness, but I did witness that this wallet might have fallen out of someone's pocket." He opened it to reveal the driver's license, and asked, "Are you Frank Gallagher?"

Frank reached back to his back pocket and didn't feel a wallet in it. "Yeah, I am, and that is my wallet."

Alice asked Christopher to come in. "This is awfully nice of you to bring it here."

"No trouble at all. I'm glad Mr. Gallagher has it back. You know what they say about a man without a wallet?"

Alice and Frank were waiting for Christopher to tell them. Frank said, "No, what do they say?"

Christopher laughed a little bit and said, "I don't know, but I thought you might know." Alice and Frank nodded and gave a courteous smile at Christopher's lame joke. "How'd you like the race?" he asked.

Alice pointed to Frank, and said, "I haven't seen him that excited for over a year." Frank sat quietly, grinned, and nodded.

"Really into racing, are you? I like it too, but the noise, and exhaust fumes, and the danger....well, it's a bit much for me."

"Frank doesn't have blood in his body. He has high-octane fuel," said Alice.

"Were you a racecar driver?"

Frank looked up at Christopher. His face was a mixture of sadness and anger. "No, I just worked on the cars."

"Worked, Frank? Frank is a master mechanic."

With an irritable edge to his word, he raised his voice and said, "Was."

"Don't get snarky with me, Frank! You *are* a master mechanic and you're wasting your life sitting in that stupid wheelchair pitying yourself." Silence prevailed.

Christopher cleared his throat and said, "Perhaps I should be going. By the way, while I'm here, I'd like to ask if you just happen to have anything you'd like to donate to Goodwill. I work there."

"Whew!" said Alice. "Anything? How about a whole bunch of auto mechanic tools that are just collecting dust?"

Frank raised his voice, and said, "Alice. Enough, please. Let's talk about this later. Yes, I do have some things I don't need anymore." He looked down at his feet, and said, "Shoes." Indy had an excellent vocabulary and recognized what Frank said. He trotted off to the bedroom and returned with a pair of shoes clenched in his mouth.

"Ha. Well I'll be," said Alice.

When Indy dropped the shoes in front of Frank, Christopher looked down on them, and said, "Hmm, they look like they are stained with oil and some grease. Are these the shoes of a master mechanic?"

"Bud, I don't know you, and I don't want to sound like I don't appreciate that you found my wallet. But my life is none of your business!"

Christopher apologized, and said, "Everyone's life is someone else's business. We are all connected. How you treat other people is very important. If you give to others you reward yourself. You know what they say, and this is one I do know, *what goes around, comes around*." Again, there was silence.

Alice broke the silence. "I'm sorry about all of this. Can I get you a cup of coffee? Would you like to sit awhile?"

Christopher accepted her offer of coffee, and sat on the lounge chair next to Frank. Uncharacteristically, Indy sat next to Christopher, not Frank. Alice delivered the coffee and also took a seat. "I assume you had an accident of some kind, and you don't have use of your legs anymore," said Christopher.

"You got that right," said Frank.

"May I ask what's been keeping you busy since the accident? Hobbies, charitable works, volunteering?"

Frank sat still. He could have said *no, no, no* to Christopher's questions. He could have said mostly *watching stock car races on TV.* He could have opened-up about his dreams and his misery to get it out of his heart and off his chest. He chose not to say any of that, and said, "Not much, really."

Frank kept rubbing his hands together, staring at the ceiling fan as it slowly twirled. Christopher sensed Frank was going through introspection about where he was and where he is in life. He took the chance to give Frank a penetrating thought. "Frank, look at me." Frank did. He saw a kind face that bespoke a caring nature. "You can't walk, but you can step forward with your life."

For the third time there was silence in the family room. Indy whimpered. Christopher knew why, but accepted what Alice said: "Yes, I'll get you some left-over steak, Indy."

Christopher told them that he had to get going, sat up, and then said, "Remember that old saying, *Shoes make the man"*

"I thought it was *clothes,"* said Frank.

"Well that too. Bye bye."

Alice told Frank that she thought she saw Christopher at church when that raffle thing was going on. "Coincidence," said Frank.

"Yeah, I guess so. Nice man. Nice advice, no?"

"Yeah, nice man." As Alice was clearing the cups and dinner plates, and then giving Indy some steak, Frank grabbed the remote and pointed it at the TV. He didn't press any buttons because he was thinking about what

Christopher said. He reached for his coffee and saw the ticket stubs on the side table. He called out to Alice to come to him. "Alice, what's the ticket number on these tickets?"

She looked at the stubs and said, "1007 and 1008. So?"

"1007 is October 7th. That's the day of my accident. 1008 is October 8th."

"Your birthday, Frank. Now that's what I call a coincidence."

———————————

Weeks later, Alice arrived at Frank's carrying a helium balloon. "It's Tuesday, Alice. At least I think it is. What are you doing here?"

She tied the balloon string to Frank's wheelchair. Indy looked at the balloon and barked. "Hey, Frank. The dog is wishing you a happy birthday."

"Very funny. Yeah, a happy birthday that's not so happy."

"Gotta tell ya, Frank. You look pretty good for a 40-year-old."

"I know I'm 40, but I feel like 80."

"I'll stick with 40 if you don't mind." She then went into the kitchen while Frank was watching TV.

Indy barked when he heard footsteps approaching the front door. Alice knew who was coming. She went to the door, opened it, and Butch McGowan was standing there with a wrapped gift in his hand. He waved to Frank from across the room. "Happy birthday, Frank!"

Frank was speechless for a moment. Butch shook Alice's hand and whispered, "Great idea. They'll be here soon."

———

Frank wheeled towards Butch, and greeted him with a cordial, but not very enthusiastic handshake. "Long time, Butch. Have a seat. Beer?"

"Sure" Alice went into the kitchen, got two beers, and gave them to Butch and Frank. "Thanks, Alice," said Butch, "and again, happy birthday my old friend." They clinked their beer bottles and took a swig.

Indy barked again. Alice opened the front door and five guys, all past crew members from Frank's team, screamed out, "Happy birthday!" Frank was beside himself. He didn't know if he should laugh or cry. He just sat there, kind of smiling, numb. Alice made everyone comfortable in the family room. She served them beers and passed around a snack tray she prepared earlier. There was lots of chit chat going on, guys ribbing guys about their sex life or idiosyncratic mannerisms. Anyone could tell by the laughter that all the guys were good friends.

Alice lit 40 candles on the birthday cake and carried it to the family room. She semi-sung the cue for them to start singing, and they did. Frank looked at the 40 candles, knowing it was his duty to at least pretend to make a wish. He didn't pretend. His unspoken wish was to have a life again. The guys saw Frank's chest expand when he took a giant breath. He blew so hard that the wind unplanted several candles. "That must be one helluva wish, Frank," said one of his ex-crewmates.

Butch handed Frank his birthday present. Slowly opening it, Frank looked around, smiling at each one of the six guys at his birthday gathering. The only thing inside the box was an envelope. Frank assumed it was a birthday card, maybe having some cash in it. He held the envelope and thanked everyone for coming. Butch said, "Open it."

It was a card, as Frank guessed, but void of money. The cover of the card was a photo of all 12 guys that worked with Frank as mechanics on McGowan's cars. "Great photo," said Frank.

"Open the card, Frank!" said Butch.

Frank opened it. He was stunned by what he read.

You taught us. We became better because of you. We still need more teaching. Come back, Frank.

Tears rolled down Frank's face. He wiped them with his sleeve. Words were dancing in his head, but his mouth didn't know how to say them. He opened his arms and reached out, inviting all of the guys for a group hug. He had absolute joy in his heart. He thought to himself... *Glad you didn't take my shoes, Christopher.*

K en Roman pondered if he should face the issue burning in his mind or forget about it. If he raised the question, the answer could bring unbeliev- able comfort, so he decided to confront Christopher. Two seconds later, he thought questioning him could *upset the applecart,* so he decided to not talk to Christopher. *Yes, no, yes, no* went his thoughts.

Ken saw how Christopher, an elderly man with shiny white hair, gentle blue eyes, and a kind-looking face, treated Goodwill customers. As store manager, he witnessed how customers responded to his words and actions. He saw people coming into the store, looking like average, normal people. When they left, they seemed happier. They seemed to walk taller with a renewed spirit. He saw children's eyes light up when Christopher would show them a dress, or toy, or a pair of shoes. He witnessed a homeless person tak- ing charge of his life and changing it for the better. He saw sympatico strangers that met because they both encountered Christopher.

He's a magician, thought Ken. *Merlin reincarnated? An altruistic alien that has come to earth to help us?* For several weeks Ken tried to make heads or tails out of who Christopher really was.

Spending a few minutes straightening donated

books in the book racks, Ken saw a leather-bound book entitled *"Angels – Real or Conjured?"* The cover depicted a man, an ordinary looking human being. In the background were representations of heavenly-looking objects – a crucifix, cherubs, wings, and halo. Ken decided to not rack the book, and took it to his office to skim through the pages. As he did, his mind steered him in the direction of *Real.* He thought, *If I don't talk to Christopher, I'll be haunted by my suspicions.*

Christopher arrived bright and early at Goodwill. In his typical high-spirited manner, he greeted his co-workers, wishing them a good morning and a blessed day. Ken put his arm around Christopher's shoulders, and said, "I need to talk with you about something before we open our doors."

"By all means, Ken."

Ken walked with Christopher, his arm still around his shoulders. He escorted him into his small, humble office at the back of the store. "Please have a seat, my friend."

Christopher sat on the only guest chair in the office. Ken sat at his desk chair. With folded fingers he leaned across his desk toward Christopher. With a quiet tone, he said, "Today is your one-year anniversary with us, and I must compliment you for the fabulous work you've done."

"Well, thank you Ken. That's very kind of you to say." Ken unfolded his fingers and sat back. "I need to know something, and I hope my question doesn't offend you."

"I'm not easily offended. In fact, I'm never offended. Ask away, Ken."

Stammering, Ken asked, "Uh...are you...ah...are you an angel?"

Christopher stayed perfectly calm, and uttered a slight giggle. He could not lie, but he had to resist saying *yes.* He answered Ken with a non-answer. "Most, if not all Christians, believe in angels."

"It's okay, Christopher. You don't have to hide it. I'm a man of faith. I believe in angels. A renewed belief, you might say. I think God sends angels to earth to help us in our time of need. That's what you have done since you've been here for the last year. You have helped Goodwill, and you have helped many, many people."

This time Christopher folded his fingers and leaned forward. "Ken, I admire the work you do here. Your commitment. I not only respect you, I like you very much. But if there was another person in this room listening to you, well, they just might say you're off your rocker."

Ken laughed out loud, and then became dead-serious as he again folded his fingers, leaned forward, and spoke to Christopher in an almost whisper-like voice. "I know you're not allowed to say anything about being an angel. I mean, I'm guessing you're not allowed. But it's okay." Christopher just shook his head. "I'm also guessing that you're not allowed to lie, so tell me, Christopher, are you an angel?"

"Here's an analogy for you, Ken. Doctors help people who get injured, like putting a bandage on their cut. If I put a bandage on someone's cut, would that make me a doctor?"

Ken nodded several times as he thought about Christopher's question. "No, that doesn't make you a doctor, but it could also be true that you *are* a doctor."

Christopher pinched his cheeks and held a smile. "See, skin. And inside this skin are bones. If you put your hand on my heart, you'd feel it beating. No wings.

No halo on my head, and I don't know how to play the harp."

"And how about the spirit that lives inside you?"

"Ken, Ken, Ken. What can I say?"

"You haven't answered my question, Christopher. Yes or no? Are you an angel?"

Christopher was concerned that Ken would tell people what he believed, and that could conceivably cause a problem for Christopher as well as the other staffers. He closed his eyes and tried to get guidance from heaven, even though he was told that he was on his own when he became an angel. He needed to decide, and did. "Ken, I am going to tell you a story."

———— ✦ ————

Christopher recounted his years on a farm in Oklahoma, which, in the early 1860s, was known as the Indian Territory. "There were many tribes living next to each other in what were called *nations*. My farm happened to be near the Choctaw Nation."

He told Ken about his childhood friend, Achukma. "We were ten years old the first time we saw each other. I was playing in the woods, chasing squirrels. Achukma was gathering kindling to take to his parents. We immediately bonded. I helped him with the kindling, and he joined me in chasing squirrels." Christopher's face nearly glowed as he thought back to those childhood years. "It didn't matter what game we played, we always had fun. Sometimes we laughed so hard that our stomachs hurt."

Christopher was accepted by Achukma's parents

as part of his family. "They called me *Na Hullo.* It means white boy." Achukma was likewise accepted by Christopher's parents. "They called him *Son* to reinforce their acceptance of him."

When they were 12-years-old, Christopher suggested that they become blood brothers. Achukma made a small incision on his palm. Christopher followed suit. They clasped their hands and raised their arms to the sky. Blood mixed with blood, and it coagulated in their hearts. They loudly declared that they would be blood brothers forever. "I still have that little scar," said Christopher, as he turned his hand and showed Ken.

Christopher talked about how he and his blood brother were very much the same, and how they were much different. "Achukma had a bow and arrows; I had a slingshot and stones. Achukma always shot at a tree or other inanimate objects. I shot at birds and squirrels. Sometimes at deer." A couple of years later, Achukma practiced with his tomahawk; Christopher practiced with the 1841 Mississippi musket his father gave to him. The weapons changed, but the targets didn't. "Achukma didn't want to kill anything unless it was for food or to be used for clothing. I had a different point of view. You could say *I was out for blood.*"

The Civil War broke out. Achukma and Christopher had both turned 16-years-old. Achukma did not want to fight, but his father said it was his duty. The Choctaw thought the Confederates would win the war, and that they would, therefore, have a better chance to protect their sovereignty as an Indian nation. Christopher wanted to fight. Because his father was against slavery, Christopher took his advice to join the Union Army. Both young men lived through the various battles and skirmishes. Both had suffered hunger when food supplies were depleted. Both managed to survive bitter cold winters.

Achukma did not kill any Union soldiers, but he did protect his fellow soldiers and helped them if they were wounded. Christopher was a fighter. He put a tiny notch on his gunstock every time he killed or wounded a Confederate. "I was 18-years-old, Ken. I served for two years in the Union Army and had lots of notches on my gunstock."

"On July 17, 1863, my brigade was ordered to defend the impending onslaught of Confederate soldiers at Honey Springs. I looked forward to fighting. As far as I was concerned, the gray coats were my enemy. They were faceless. They were birds and squirrels to me."

Christopher paused. His head bowed, and it seemed he was on the verge of crying. He cleared his throat and continued to tell his story. "It was raining. You couldn't see very far. They came at us. I fired. I thought I hit one of them. I reloaded and took aim again, but froze."

Christopher closed his eyes and looked somber as he relived the incident in his mind. He regained his composure, and continued with his story. "Captain Bluth kicked me in the leg and told me to shoot. I couldn't. I saw that my target was an Indian. I thought it might be Achukma. Bluth again told me to fire. I aimed high to avoid hitting anyone. He kicked me again and my finger squeezed the trigger. I realized I didn't aim high enough. My shot hit the Indian and he fell." Christopher stopped speaking.

Ken correctly surmised that the memory Christopher was recalling upset him. "We could take a break, but If you're up to it, I would like to hear more of your story."

Christopher complied. He told Ken that after the battle was over, and the Union Army won, he and his fellow soldiers went into the field to help any wounded Union soldiers. "The Indian I thought might have been Achukma, was Achukma. He was barely alive. I knelt down, crying, telling him that I was sorry, and hoping that he would live. I never prayed to God before that day, but I did as I knelt next to my blood brother."

"He died while you were next to him?"

"Yes. But before he died, he talked to me. He forgave me because he knew I was doing what I had to do, just like he did what he had to do. He reminded me of what his name means in Choctaw. It means peace. He grabbed my forearm with his bloody hand. He looked at me and said, 'You are my brother. Learn peace. Walk in my shoes,' and then he died."

Christopher again paused, vividly recalling how he felt. "I carried Achukma for a mile back to the Confederates camp. I was surrounded by soldiers pointing their guns at me, but they didn't fire. They saw that I was grieving the loss of one of their soldiers." Christopher laid Achukma's body on the ground. "I looked up to the soldiers and said I was sorry. I'm sure they understood."

He told Ken that he took Achukma's moccasins. "I kept them for all of my life. My human life."

———————— ⁕ ————————

"Unbelievable, Christopher. I mean, I believe you, but your story...well, your story is incredible." Christopher was expressionless. "So, then what, Christopher?"

Christopher said he stopped killing people. He asked to be reassigned to the food wagon, and was very thankful that Captain Bluth allowed it. "I took an oath when I joined the Army, and I had to live-up to my promise. Thankfully, the oath did not say *kill,* just *serve.*"

When the war ended, Christopher returned home to his farm. His parents had suffered during the war years, as did most families, but remained healthy, and most importantly, were alive. He worked the farm with his father, and found great joy in tilling soil and growing crops. He would smell the corn he shucked before giving it to his mother for her to cook. "When I smelled it, I had a wonderful feeling that I did something important by growing it. I felt I gave it life, and it rewarded me by giving me food. My crops and I had a symbiotic relationship."

Christopher spent all of his remaining years on earth giving life, so to speak, to others. He married and had three children. He and his father, along with the help of several neighbors, built a church. Christopher became its minister and preached the word of God. He worked tirelessly as a minister, a husband, a father, and a farmer. He gave his all to whomever needed guidance or help – physical or spiritual. "So that's my story, Ken. I died when I was 55-years-old."

Ken gulped. "Died? I can't wrap my head around this. You died and then became alive again? You mean you went to heaven, right?"

"Yes, I did."

There was a knock on the door. Ken said, "Come in." Corina opened the door, kept her hand on the doorknob, leaned in, and said, "Five minutes to opening, Ken. We're all set."

"Thank you, Corina. We'll be out in just a moment."
The door closed. Ken said, "I must know about heaven.
Please sit tight. I'll be back in a minute. Ken went to the
men's room and splashed cold water on his face. He
slapped both of his cheeks and talked to himself in the
mirror. "Holy moly. He *is* an angel."

"So where were we? Ah, yes, you asked if I went to
heaven."

Christopher knew that Ken's emotions were running at break-neck speed, and he was on the verge of
bouncing off the walls. He wanted to lighten the conversation. He let out a huge laugh, and said, "To answer
your question, 'Did I go to heaven?' Hell, yes! I went
to heaven." Ken looked shocked. "Sorry, I just couldn't
resist that little play on words." He told Ken that he was
reunited with Achukma, as if they never left each other.
"It was glorious being together with him."

"And your wife and children?"

"When they died, they joined me in heaven."

"If my math is right, you were in heaven for about
100 years. Right?"

"Funny you should say that, Ken."

Christopher told him that he was called into the
Divine Chambers to meet with one of the head angels
who told him that it was time to move on. "You've been
here for 100 years, Christopher. Happy anniversary!"
said the head angel.

Christopher told the head angel that he felt like he
was in heaven for only a few days, a week at most.

The head angel told him that heaven's calendar is a bit different from earth's calendar. As he told me, "Infinity is a very long time. If we kept an earth-like calendar up here, it would take us forever to write down what year it was." Christopher smiled, thinking that his description of heavenly-time was amusing. Ken didn't react. He took everything Christopher said as gospel.

"There are anniversaries in heaven?"

"Heaven is very much like earth. We angels joke that living in heaven is like heaven on earth, but in heaven." Ken still sat quietly, again not reacting to Christopher's joke.

Christopher cleared his throat, and said, "So, the head angel told me that it's traditional for us *One Hundred Years in Heaven* folks to have an opportunity to go back to earth, as a human, but only if we wanted to."

Ken said, "Aha, so you agreed to come back."

"Yes. I came back to earth, as a human...well, a human of sorts, one year ago today."

Ken appeared hypnotized. He had a blank look on his face. His eyes were focused on Christopher.

"So there you have it, Ken. You were right. I am an angel."

"It's fascinating and I must say, a little scary. I was convinced that you were an angel, but now that I absolutely, positively know that you are, I just don't know what else I can say."

"You don't have to say anything, Ken. I'm glad I told you about myself. It's a relief in some ways. You know, of course, that you can't tell anyone."

"Absolutely not. As you said before, they would think I'm off my rocker."

Christopher extended his hand to shake Ken's. When their hands clasped, Christopher looked upward and spoke to the heavens through his thoughts. *You of course know that I told him, and you know why. If I am dismissed as an angel, please help Ken deal with what I told him.*

Christopher said, "I am confident that you will not tell anyone." Ken smiled. He didn't feel that his hand became warmer, or that a shiver travelled up through his whole body. Christopher felt the same sensations and smiled. His thought to the heavens was *Thank you.* His words to Ken were, "So, Ken. What did you want to see me about?"

"Ahh, oh, I know. I wanted to wish you a happy anniversary." Christopher opened the office door. Corina happened to be approaching it to tell Ken that the store was open. Ken said, "Corina, today is Christopher's one year anniversary with us."

Corina said, "Yes, indeed. Happy anniversary. You've been a godsend."

"What a glorious weekend, Paul. I want to live in these trees so I can be surrounded by all this beautiful color all the time."

"Well, if you want to squirrel-away, I'll let you out now." Paul and Kelly smiled at Paul's pun.

"Stop, Paul."

"I was only kidding about the squirrel. Besides, I don't have my ladder so you'll have to climb up the branches."

She slapped his arm, and told him to pull over. She pointed toward the farmland behind the split-rail fence. "There. I just saw a guy fall down."

When Paul and Kelly got to the fallen man, he was holding his leg and trying to mask his pain. "Can we help you?"

"Nah. Thanks. Just a bad fall. I'll be fine." He started to get up and fell down again, holding his leg. "Well, I got that wrong. I think I might have broken something."

"We'll call 911 and get you some help. In the meantime, I think I can help you a little. I'm an EMT with the fire department."

"I live just over there. If you help me get there, I'd appreciate it. This ground is a bit wet and muddy."

Kelly rigged a field-torniquet with a tree branch and Paul's belt. With a fireman's carry, Paul delivered him to his house. He knocked on the front door, and his passenger called out, "Vera, open up."

When Vera opened the door, he said, "Slipped in the mud. Probably broke something."

"And who are you, young man?"

"I'm Paul, Paul Hanson. This is my wife Kelly."

"Glad you were there to help him. Can you please lay Noah down on his bed? Right this way."

While Paul and Vera were helping Noah, Kelly looked around their living room. She was drawn to the curio cabinet and felt admiration when she saw the collection of small shiny sculptures. Vera came back from the bedroom, and said, "Do you believe in destiny?"

"Sometimes."

"Well, I do. I think it was destiny that you two happened to be there when Noah fell."

"Yes, I can see what you mean," said Kelly. "We really should call 911. I'm a nurse and can tell that he will need medical attention.

"Vera said, "Those ambulance people charge a lot of money. I'll take him myself. If you could just help me get him in the back of our pick-up, I'd appreciate that."

They agreed to help. Kelly kept looking at the collection while Vera was getting her coat. "Nice, no? I've been collecting those for years. Mostly Hummel and Lladró. Some I don't know, but I like them all."

"I'm mesmerized by that shoe. It's absolutely gorgeous. Look at all that detail," said Kelly.

Vera took the miniature porcelain shoe out of the case and handed it to Kelly. "Yeah, it's a beaut, alright. But I don't like it as much as the little people. I'll tell you what. I want to thank both of you for helping us. I think you would be offended if I offered you money, and besides, we ain't got much of that. You keep it."

Kelly held the shoe, almost caressing it, and said, "No, no, no. I can't accept this. It's part of your collection."

Vera responded with, "And now you are part of my collection, my collection of people I've met with a good heart. Noah, let's go take a ride to the hospital."

———— ◦◉◦ ————

Kelly started her work day as a dialysis nurse in a very good mood. She had a great weekend with her husband, helped a man in need, and got a beautiful porcelain sculpture that she prominently displayed in her home.

Wendy Muller was her first patient. She liked Wendy. They were about the same age, and seemed to have several common interests. In many ways they were simpatico. "Hey, Wendy. How you doin' today?"

"Like two days ago, and like the two days before that, and, you know."

"Yes, I do know. Let's get you hooked-up. Are you doing earbuds, reading, or do you want to chit-chat a bit?"

"Earbuds and a book. I'm going to listen to romantic music while I read Clayton's new romance novel that takes place during the Civil War."

"I bet there are a bunch of great sex scenes in the book."

Wendy laughed, waved her hand at Kelly, and said, "Pshaw. I just like history." Once Wendy was hooked-up to the dialysis machine, and her earbuds were snug in her ears, Kelly laid a blanket across her lap, handed her her book, and wiggled her fingers to signal *See you later.*

The day proceeded without incident. Her dialysis patients all seemed to be fine, all reading or watching TV or sleeping. Kelly skipped out to have lunch in the hospital cafeteria. She sat down at a long table which was occupied by an elderly man. "Good ham and cheese sandwich, isn't it?" he said.

Kelly lifted the half of a sandwich she was holding, and waved it at the man while nodding in agreement. He held up his sandwich, pointed to it, and then at Kelly's sandwich, and nodded, essentially telling her that they both had ham and cheese sandwiches.

Kelly noticed a book on the table. The cover had a photograph of a little boy playing a fiddle. It was a figurine. The title of the book was, "Hummel – The History." Kelly was intrigued by the coincidence. "Sir, please excuse my asking, but I'm very curious. Why do you have that book?"

Christopher pointed to the book, and said, "This book? Why, it's just a book about history, and I like history. Why are you asking?" Kelly related the story of the injured farmer and the figurine she was given. "Yes, it is quite a coincidence, isn't it?" Christopher opened the book at the bookmark, and said, "I just learned that you can trace the history of these figurines by the trademark, the foundry, and the sculptor that made them. It's all at the bottom of the piece."

"Interesting," said Kelly. She looked at her watch, and said, "Break is over. Gotta get back to my patients. Nice meeting you."

Christopher looked at her name badge, and said, "Indeed. I'm Christopher, and it was nice meeting you, Nurse Kelly Hanson."

⸺⸺◆⸺⸺

Paul walked into the living room when he got home from his shift, gave Kelly a kiss on the cheek, and asked, "How was your day?"

"Interesting, fascinating, confusing, beneficial, and, you know, fine."

"What are you searching for on the Internet?"

"Figurines."

He took his jacket off, and headed to the kitchen. "I'm getting a beer. Want anything?"

"No, I'm okay." When he returned with his beer, he looked over her shoulder at the computer monitor. "I'm trying to figure out what the markings on the bottom of my shoe are. You know, the porcelain shoe that Vera gave me. Right now, it's like hieroglyphics. Goethel, 1969, B.W. 17/90."

"I'd really like to help, but the game's on." He walked over to the sofa, turned the TV on, and put his feet on the coffee table. His eyes were glued to the TV monitor; Kelly's eyes were glued to the computer monitor.

The evening wore on. The game ended, nearly all of the pizza they had delivered was eaten, and they relaxed in side-by-side recliners in the backyard, looking at the stars without any need to talk. "I can't wait," she said.

"Honey, I had a long day. Actually, a long three days at the firehouse. Would you mind..."

She interrupted him, grabbed and squeezed his knee as she got up from the recliner, and said, "Sweetheart. I know you're dying to get me into bed and take care of your animal instincts." She started to laugh. "But I think you need to rest a bit. I'm going back to my research." She kissed him on his forehead, and went back into the house, closed the screen door, but kept the patio door opened to air-out the house.

It was a chilly autumn night. Paul threw a blanket over himself and closed his eyes for a moment. The moment turned into several hours, during which time Kelly clicked on many websites, trying to decipher the apparent Egyptian etchings at the bottom of her porcelain shoe. She screamed out, "Yes!"

Paul's body lifted from the recliner as if an earthquake hit. It took him a couple of seconds to realize that the noise he heard was Kelly's exuberance. He went inside and saw Kelly raising and lowering her desk chair as she anxiously waited for the printer to print. "I'm guessing that you're happy about your shoe thingy. Right?"

"You're a good guesser, Mr. Fireman. They're not hieroglyphics. The shoe was made by the Goethel Foundry in Stuttgart, Germany in 1969. The 17 slash 90 means this was the 17th one that was made out of the lot of 90. Isn't it strange that my birthday is on the 17th and I was born in 1990? The B.W. was the artist's name, the sculptor's name. It was Barnim Weber." Kelly looked at Paul, waiting for him to say something. He shrugged his shoulders. She repeated "Weber! My maiden name is Weber."

"Who's Barnim?"

"I don't know, but think about it, Paul."

"Hmm. Interesting. Quite a coincidence. But Weber is a fairly common name."

"This is the third coincidence I had today. Three co-incidences in one day, when they're all connected, it's not a coincidence. It's a...I don't know what it is, but a bee is buzzing in my bonnet and I have to find out why."

=====◀◀◉▶▶=====

Kelly couldn't wait for her shift to be over. She was obsessed with the coincidences. Trying to con-nect the dots, she thought *Wendy likes history, that guy Christopher likes history, the shoe was made by Barnim Weber, my name is Weber.* She walked down the hallway to check on her patients, and it dawned on her. *Noah and Vera are the connection. It has to be.* She stopped in her tracks, and whispered to herself, "I'm going to get to the bottom of this."

That evening, Kelly told Paul that she needed to go back to Noah's and Vera's house to talk with them. "It's nice that you want to check-up on the old guy, but you can call them to see how he's doing."

"I don't know their last name, and I don't have their number. Besides, I'd rather talk face-to-face. It's not about his leg, it's about the coincidences."

"I can't go this weekend. My shift's Friday to Sunday."

"I'll just drive up there myself. It's not that far. I'll get a chance to see the trees again"

Paul gave her a hug, letting her know that he agreed, supporting her need to figure out what's go-ing on. He knew she'd be disappointed when the coincidence turned out to be a simple coincidence, but thought it better that she discovered that. He yawned a giant yawn and stretched out his arms. "Coming to bed, babe?"

"I'm still a little wound-up. I'm going to have a night-cap and watch whatever boring movie I can find. Kissy kissy."

She took her glass of wine from the kitchen and went to turn on the TV, passing by the computer. It binged to signal that she had a message. She sat down to see that the message was an ad from an art gallery, announcing an exhibit of fine art and rare sculptures. She thought, *Boy, you can't sneeze these days without those folks in cyberspace saying bless you.* And then she thought, *What the heck, why not?* She did an Internet search for Goethel Foundry. When the list appeared, she clicked on 'sculptors' and found a listing of three men, one of whom was Barnim Weber. She then searched Barnim Weber. A long list of websites appeared, all of them ads, except for one that had the words *Family Records Germany.* Click. She read the topical information about him, and then spilled her wine on the keyboard as she bolted back from her desk. "Oh my God!" she yelled. She ran upstairs to tell Paul, but he was sleeping and she didn't want to wake him. *I'll tell him the great news in the morning*, she thought. The wine that she drank did its trick. She undressed and got into bed.

———— ((○)) ————

Bright and early, Kelly went downstairs to the kitchen to have morning coffee with Paul. She looked forward to knocking his socks off with what she found out. Paul wasn't there, but his note was. It read: *"It's 4 a.m. Had to get to the station. Back home about 10."* Kelly had to be at work by eight, so she made coffee, ate a piece of left-over cold pizza, and got ready for work.

"Good morning, my favorite patient."

Wendy replied, "Good morning, my favorite nurse who jabs me with things." Both of them smiled, and then did a fist bump.

"I know you'll probably want to read your book, but if you don't mind, I'd like to bend your ear with a little story. Actually, not a story. A real thing."

Wendy welcomed hearing Kelly's story, and Kelly proceeded to tell her about the coincidences, and then her discovery last night. "My great grandfather was Dietrick Weber. His brother's name was Barnim. My maiden name is Weber. I think Barnim Weber is my great granduncle.

Wendy listened attentively to Kelly's story. She was agape when Kelly mentioned her revelation about Barnim. "Kelly, sorry, I have something to do. Can I come back in an hour?"

"Well, sure, Wendy. Our chairs aren't filled today, so there's no problem delaying dialysis for an hour." Wendy put her shoes back on and scooted out.

An hour later Wendy was back at the hospital. She sat in her chair and was greeted, again, by Kelly. "All set now?"

"Not really, but it will be set."

"Huh?"

Wendy pulled out a wrapped item from her large canvas bag and slowly unwrapped it.

When the item was revealed, Kelly's eyes and

mouth popped open. She had difficulty talking, and said, "What the...what? How? I don't...what?"

"Does yours look like mine?" asked Wendy.

"Yeah. Identical."

Wendy turned it over and read what was on the bottom of her figurine. "Goethel, 1969, B.W. 1 of 90." She handed the shoe to Kelly. Kelly's eyes were still lit as she held it. She had the same feeling that she had when she held it for the first time at Vera's house.

"Kelly, my maiden name is also Weber. Your great granduncle is my great grandfather."

They hugged, they cried, they felt a connection only two people who love each other could feel.

———⊰⊙⊱———

When Kelly arrived at home, she told Paul what happened. He couldn't believe it, but he did believe it. He wrapped his arms around Kelly, giving her a warm, giant hug. "That's the most incredible thing I ever heard."

Kelly said, "I now believe in destiny."

Paul said, "And I believe there's more to coincidences than a coincidence."

Kelly asked Paul to sit down because she wanted to tell him something. "Uh oh, is this one of those *we have to talk* talks?"

"Not at all. It's a match."

"What's a match?"

"Wendy and me. I had it checked out before I left the hospital. Wendy doesn't know yet. I'm going to her house tonight to tell her that I am donating a kidney to her."

He Nailed It

'll give it until I'm 18 and then I'm out of here, thought David Callan as he walked around his family's non-working farmland. His parents bought the 10-acre farm so they could say goodbye to a smog-ridden city and live in the country – so they said. That was a year ago. They had no intention of working the land – they weren't farmers. Their intention, as David found out in years to come, was to raise him in a better environment, one that could get the tough, street-smart kid away from crime and probable harm. He was *mixing with the wrong element,* as his father would tell his new neighbors.

The Callans were delighted with their new environment. Fresh air, openness, and surrounded by friendly and caring people – the kind of people you envision that live in a small rural town. David was not delighted. He liked the hustle and bustle of the city. He liked the crowd of boys that he hung out with, even though he knew that they were up to no-good more often than not. He wanted to be part of a gang so he could feed his ego with a sense of being superior. All of that was taken away when he moved.

He was bored in the country. During his first semester in his new high school, he was the outcast, the city kid. He didn't realize at the time that he brought that on himself. He shunned friendly gestures from his classmates, thinking they were a bunch of hicks, below him in the social order. He kept to himself, never socializing after class got out. He would start his senior year in September. He dreaded the thought of spending summer months in the country with nothing to do.

———((O))———

"Uh oh!" yelled Christopher from the other side of the split-rail fence that was between the farm and two-lane, asphalt road.

David looked up to see an old man on a bicycle who lost control and was about to fall. David just watched, not having any interest in trying to help him right his bike. "Whew," said Christopher. Almost fell." He got off his bike and picked up a small object from the road. "Yours?" he asked David.

David approached him, and asked, "What is it?"

"A horseshoe. Looks like I got lucky. This nail could have punctured my tire."

"Must have been a helluva throw," David said, as he laughed and totally disregarded Christopher's remarks.

"Oh, you mean horseshoes, as in the game. Yes, that's funny. Have you ever played horseshoes?"

David put his hands in his pocket, which Christopher saw as an emotionally defensive posture. He knew about David's background, and knew that David was not one to make idle conversation, or necessarily care about other people. "Nah. It's a sissy game."

Christopher looked at the horseshoe, and said, "Want this, or should I throw it away so it can puncture someone else's tire?"

With a smirk, David said, "Throw it away." Christopher didn't respond with either words or actions, but stood silent, hoping David would reconsider what he said.

David did. "Hey, forget it. I'll take it."

"Good." Christopher handed it to him. "Watch out for that nail."

David took the horseshoe from him and looked at it. It was the first time he ever held one. He wondered why it had a nail in it, and why it was on the road. Christopher said, "I wonder why it has a nail in it, and why it was on the road."

David looked up at him, showing absolute surprise on his face. "Are you a mind reader? That's exactly what I was thinking."

"I guess great minds think alike." Christopher sat on the fence, wanting to have a friendly chat that he thought just might steer David to a discovery.

"I like mysteries. Do you?"

"Yeah, I guess so. I like to figure out who the killer is before the movie ends. I hate it when you know who the killer is right at the beginning, unless there's a lot of action. You know, fights, Kung Fu, all that stuff."

"Well, here's a mystery for you. Sorry, there's no killer in it. Both of us had the same questions about that horseshoe. Why is there a nail in it? And why was it on the road?"

David contemplated the questions. He looked at the horseshoe and he looked at Christopher. He shrugged his shoulders, and said, "I don't know."

"Hmm," said Christopher. You look like a very smart kid. I bet you could find out if you really wanted to. I bet you could solve the mystery."

"What do I get if I figure it out?"

"Self-respect."

"Huh?"

"Sorry, lad. It's time for me to go." Christopher hopped on his bike and peddled off. David watched him ride away, and looked at the horseshoe again. It *was* a mystery as to why it was on the road, especially because it had a nail in it. *Maybe I'll find out and tell that old guy he was right about me being smart.*

≡◉≡

"It's about time you came down. Breakfast or lunch?" asked his mother when David decided to get out of bed and join the family at half past ten.

"Breakfast."

"Did I hear a *please*?"

David yawned, and said, "Breakfast, please, my most wonderful mother." His mother heard the sarcasm in his tone, but elected to not start an argument, especially in the morning of a beautiful summer Saturday.

"What are you going to do today?"

"I don't know. Maybe feed the chickens and the pigs, and toss hay to the cattle."

"Very funny, David. I'll be sure to tell your dad that we should buy some livestock so you can do your chores like a good farmer boy." David rolled his eyes.

He got dressed, put the horseshoe in his backpack, and set off for the two-mile bike ride to town. He thought the best way to find out about the horseshoe was to ask someone who knows about horseshoes.

He arrived at Cal's Hardware, showed Cal the

horseshoe, and asked, "Got any idea where this came from?"

Cal said, "Probably off the wall above someone's front door."

"I found it on the road."

"Hmm. That changes things. I don't know much if anything about horseshoes, but I know someone who knows everything about them." Cal wrote *Abner Bent* on a piece of paper, as well as directions to his home, and handed the paper to David. "Abner's a blacksmith. You should ask him."

"Okay."

"I never saw you before. You new here?"

"Yeah. Moved here a year ago."

"Welcome, son."

David set-off to see Abner Bent. During his bike ride he gave thought to Cal welcoming him. He never heard that kind of thing from anyone while he lived in the city.

When he arrived at Bent's place, he saw a large man, over six feet tall and weighing at least 300 pounds. He had an unusual looking black cap that covered only part of his long, gray hair that was speckled with ashes. His curly, gray beard covered half of his face, and it too was speckled with ash. He cut a menacing figure, even to the tough, street-smart city kid.

"Hey! Are you Bent?"

Abner laid down his straight peen hammer, and walked away from his anvil. He took his glove off his right hand, extended it to David, and said, "I'm Mr. Bent, but you can call me Abner. How can I help you today?"

"David." He was pleasantly surprised by Abner's greeting. Had he seen Abner in the city, he would have walked on the other side of the street. Here, in Abner's barn-like workshop, David felt at ease with the man. He handed Abner the horseshoe and explained how and where it was found. "Can you tell me anything about this?"

"Sure can. First of all, it's pretty new. Wasn't worn very much by the horse. You can still see the markings."

"What markings?"

Abner pointed to the "M," telling him that it was made by a company called Mustad; he pointed to the "1," and said, "This size is for sure for a small horse, maybe a pony."

"What about the nail?" asked David.

"Son, as they say, you hit the nail on the head." Abner explained that the shoeing was not done right. He said the nail was too short. "And look here," he said, as he pointed to the holes in the horseshoe that didn't have nails. "Only two nails were used. You can tell by the indentation in this hole, and no indentation in the other holes."

"So it fell off the horse?"

"Yup, that's what I think."

David's eyes were wide open as he listened to and watched Abner. He gained a respect for him, and felt good about being with him. They ended their conversation when Abner said, "You need to find a four-legged horse that might have a limp," and laughed so hard his belly shook.

David returned home, and sketched a route around town to find a four-legged horse with a limp.

⚬((◎))⚬

"Well, you're up early," said his mom when she glanced at the cat-with-a-swinging-tail clock on the wall. "Eight o'clock. Are you feeling okay?"

"Yeah, fine. Just hungry."

Immediately after downing two Eggo waffles and quaffing a large glass of orange juice, David hit the road to visit as many horse farms as he could find. Figuring that the horse that lost a shoe lost it on the road by his house, he biked along till he got to the first house that had horses in a corral.

He knocked on the door and was greeted by a middle-aged woman. "Can I help you, young man?"

"I found this horseshoe on the road and thought maybe it was from one of your horses."

"Why isn't that nice of you. Let's go take a look." They went to the corral where she lifted the legs of each of her three horses. "None of my horses, I'm glad to say."

"Okay. Thanks."

"Wait a minute," she called to David. I was making pancakes for my family. Would you like to join us?"

David was taken aback. He didn't knock on any strangers' doors in the city. He guessed, as many city dwellers would guess, that you don't open your door for a stranger. "That's nice of you, but I have to go. Bye."

He went to the next house that had horses. He was again greeted in a very friendly manner, and again complimented for his efforts in trying to help a horse that needed a shoe. The man that greeted him at the front door asked David if he could help him in some way. "I'm free this afternoon if you want to drive around in my pick-up." David declined the invitation, but shook the man's hand, smiled at him, and said he needed the exercise on his bike.

And so it went for the next six houses he visited. Everyone was very nice to him, very cooperative. At the ninth house he was not only thanked, he was invited to play basketball with a group of guys, all of whom were about his age, three of whom were in his class. "Come on, we could use another player," said one of his classmates.

David was beside himself. He spewed derogatory remarks at some of the guys when he saw them in school, and here they were being friendly. "Can't now. Maybe another time. Thanks."

One more house for today, he thought. He biked for another mile till he arrived at a large house that had a large corral and apparently many horses. He rang the bell. Kathy Hayden, one of his classmates, opened the door. Her head jerked up and her eyes and mouth opened, clearly showing that she was surprised. She turned her expression into a smile, and said, "Hi. You're David, right?"

"Yes. And you're…I forgot your name."

"It's Kathy. Kathy Hayseed." She looked at David and got the reaction she hoped for. He was agape and speechless. He looked like a kid caught with his pants down.

"Ah, I'm…I'm sorry I called you that."

She didn't comment on how David looked, and didn't respond to his apology, other than saying, "Hmm. Oh well." She invited him into her house. "Want something to drink?" she asked. David asked for a glass of water, which she got from the kitchen and gave it to him. "Let's sit out in the back so I can watch my horses."

"Yeah, sure. In fact, that's why I came here."

"To watch my horses?"

"No. Well, not exactly." He took the horseshoe out of his backpack and explained what happened and why he knocked on her door.

Kathy saw her father at the corral and called out to him. "Dad! David and I need a ride." Her father waved back, and held-up two fingers.

"Where are we going?" he asked.

"To the Colliers. You'll see why when we get there. Put your bike in the pick-up."

Ten minutes later he arrived at the Colliers small ranch. There was one horse, a small horse, in the small corral. Mrs. Collier was tossing hay over the corral fence. "Hi, Mrs. Collier. Can we please take a look at your horse?"

"Why, sure, Kathy. Go ahead."

In the corral, Kathy lifted the horse's leg. "No." Then another leg. "No." Then the third leg. "Hello."

"Well, I'll be," said Mrs. Colllier. "Didn't know Junior threw a shoe. He got out a few days ago. I happened to see him when he got back from wherever he was. I told Andrew to hitch that gate whenever he left the corral, but you know Andrew." She twirled her finger around at the side of her head. Kathy knew that the Colliers had one small horse, and she knew that Mr. Collier was forgetful, if not suffering with mental problems.

"I just baked a peach pie. Would you kids like a piece?"

Kathy said "Yes, that would be great."

She turned her head slightly toward David,and poked him with her elbow. David got the message and said, "Yeah. Great."

Mrs. Collier told them the peaches are as fresh as fresh can be. "Just picked them off my tree this morning."

Kathy took a forkful of her piece, and while chewing, nodded and said, "Mmm, Mmm!"

David followed suit and was genuine with his praise. "I never had peach pie before, but I think it just became my favorite." Mrs. Collier smiled in thanks.

While he ate, he not only opened his mouth to fill it with the delicious peach pie, he opened his mind to country life. He thought about the nice guy at Cal's Hardware, and the scary-looking but very friendly Abner who helped him solve the horseshoe problem. And he absolutely thought about how Kathy treated him. Had he been in the city and made fun of someone's name, they definitely would never be nice to him. Thinking about his day and the people he met, and the pie he was enjoying, he changed his perception about country life.

⟞⟝(◉)⟞⟝

As the summer progressed, David's thoughts and feelings about living in the country changed dramatically. He played basketball with the guys; he went fishing in the river with yet another group of guys; he spent many days with Kathy, at her house riding horses, and taking casual strolls in the woods talking about everything and nothing.

The more he got involved in his new town with classmates and storekeepers and several adults, the more his character changed. He started to care about people, about who they are and what they do. He lost his *I'm better than you* attitude. The summer that he dreaded became the summer that he didn't want to end.

Sitting with Kathy on a bench at the side of a jogging and bike trail, watching the runners and bicyclists going by, they waved to each and wished them a good morning. Christopher was approaching them on his bicycle. He was wearing a green hat that had a big, yellow horseshoe emblem on it. "I know that guy," said David.

"Who is he?"

"He's the guy that almost ran over that horseshoe. He challenged me to find out why it was on the road." Christopher slowed as he got closer to them. "Hey, I solved the mystery about the horseshoe," said David.

Christopher smiled as he slowly passed them, and said, "Some horseshoes are just lucky." He picked up speed, and rode off, disappearing 'round the bend.

"I think he's a leprechaun," said Kathy, as she laughed.

He also laughed, and said, "Nah, no such thing." He squinted and looked up, thinking, *Is he?*

Repurpose

C olin McGunical mumbled to himself as he unlocked the door to his little shop at the end of an old, neglected strip mall. "It's the right key, why won't it go in?" He turned the key upside down. "No, it's the other way." He tried the other two keys that were on his key chain that also sported a simple, gold wedding band.

Frustrated by not being able to open the door, he threw his keys at the lock and kicked the door. He immediately apologized to his wife. "I'm sorry, Clara. I got mad at the lock, not at you." He picked-up his keys and kissed the wedding band.

Taking a big breath to relax himself, he again inserted the key into the lock. It went in. He turned it, and the lock opened. He opened the door and clicked on the light switch. Standing at the doorway he looked around, slowly, as if he was inspecting every item in his shop. He closed his eyes and inhaled the aroma. The scent awakened his spirit to get to work.

He walked to the restroom at the back of his shop, hung-up his coat, put his flat cap on a hook, and donned his leather apron. He rubbed his hands down his chest, feeling the softness of the leather that aged for almost as many years as he had aged. "You still feel good," he said to the apron.

At the front door he flipped the sign so customers could see that he was open for business. For the last couple of years, he wondered why he bothered with the sign. He thought, *If people need my services, they'll come; if they don't, they won't.* With fewer and fewer customers passing through the door, he gave serious thought to changing the *Open* sign to *Closed for Good.*

Except for the whirring and occasional clanking of his machines, his eight-hour day at the shop was relatively quiet. Only two people came through his door on that Saturday. The first was the owner of a shop at the other end of the mall who asked Colin to sign a petition to refurbish the mall's façade. The second was a well-dressed, lovely woman who asked if she could hang a *Lost Dog* sign on his door.

Working was by far the best part of his day. He restored a pair of men's dress shoes, and a pair of knee-high leather riding boots – the only pairs on his *To be Fixed* shelf. His passion for cobbling was apparent. Although he worked for hours on the footwear, his time at cobbling never dragged. Once repaired and polished, the shoes and boots looked brand new.

He placed the shoes and boots on his *Fixed* shelf to join the other 14 pairs. Some of the 14 were collecting dust on the shelf for a month. Two pairs were there for three months.

=====◦《◎》◦=====

Clara always made a traditional Irish breakfast on Sundays, and Colin continued the tradition. He sat at his kitchen table, eating scrambled eggs with bacon,

sausage, and mushrooms, and sides of grilled toma-
toes and toast. On the opposite side of the table was
a place setting for Clara. Sipping the last of his strong
Irish Breakfast Tea, he looked out the window from his
second-floor apartment, watching people walking here
and there, some with dogs on a leash who stopped occasionally to sniff and pee. He assumed all the people
knew where they were going, but he didn't know where
he was going.

Needing a new pair of pajamas, he casually walked
a half mile to Goodwill. He was not in any rush. At the
store he looked around the various racks of shirts,
pants, and jackets, but couldn't find any pajamas. An
elderly man with white hair was setting up an oak table
and chairs. "Excuse me, sir, do you have any pajamas?" he asked Christopher.

"As a matter of fact, we do. Right this way."

Colin followed him to an area with miscellaneous
men's wear. Colin immediately eyed the shamrock
design on a pair of flannel pajamas. "Perfect." As luck
would have it, they were his size. "A double perfect."

Walking to the cashier he passed the men's shoes
display. He stopped and visually inspected the three
dozen or so pairs of gently-worn shoes, boots, and
sneakers. Christopher happened by and stood next to
him. Neither man said anything for several seconds,
then Christopher broke the ice. "Need shoes?"

"No, definitely not. I was just looking at how they
were made, and which ones could be fixed-up better."

"Fixed-up?" asked Christopher.

Colin pulled down a pair, and said, "These, for example. See how the sole is ever so slightly separated from
the upper? Needs to be re-glued." He picked-up another

pair. "And these. The stitching in the back is coming loose. It will give way, come apart, in short order."

Christopher said, "Yes, I see what you mean. You seem to know a lot about shoes. Are you a shoemaker?"

Colin replaced the shoes onto the rack. "No, I'm a cobbler. I repair shoes. Well, I should say that I *used to* repair shoes."

"So, you're retired?"

"I will soon. In fact, very soon." His eyes looked downward.

Colin and Christopher stayed at the shoe display for nearly half an hour. Christopher showed lots of interest in knowing how shoes were made, what's a good shoe and not-so-good one, and what's involved in repairing shoes. Colin answered all of Christopher's questions, sometimes long-winded with the answers. While talking, Colin painted pictures in his mind of the work he had actually done. His answers were a discourse, like the narrator in the documentaries he often watched.

"By the way, I'm Christopher."

"How'd you do. I'm Colin. Colin McGunical."

"I thought I detected a bit of an Irish brogue." They shook hands. "You have a very strong grip, Colin. And your hand feels like the leather you worked with."

With a guffaw, Colin said, "The leather's also in my veins."

Christopher looked at his watch, and said, "It's my lunch break. I'd love to hear more about cobbling, and frankly, more about you. May I buy you lunch?"

Colin put his hand on his stomach and rubbed it with a circular motion. "It's still a bit full from breakfast, but I could use another cup of tea."

"Right this way, Mr. Colin McGunical, Master Cobbler."

Christopher ordered a chef's salad; Colin had a cup of strong, very hot tea. "Tell me about yourself, Colin."

"I'm a simple man, with simple needs."

"And how did you become that?"

A decanter of hot water was placed in front of Colin, along with a cup on a saucer, and two tea bags. In his ritual manner, Colin dipped the bags into the water, took them out, dipped them in again, and let them sit. "I was born in Ireland. It seems like yesterday, but it was 66 years ago."

With a smile, Christopher said, "You've held-up well, sir. You don't look a day over 65."

"Ha! But sometimes I feel like I'm 165."

"I know that feeling."

Colin talked about his uneventful upbringing in Caryduff, Northern Ireland, a small town about ten miles from where his father worked as an engineer for an American company. "It was a grand little house. I had lots of friends, school was okay, I played a lot of sports, you know, I did all the things kids do. I look back and I remember being a pretty happy kid."

"But things changed, didn't they?"

"Yes, indeed. When I was a young teenager, everyone in town wondered what was going to happen with all that disagreement the Irish had with the Brits. Do you know about that?"

Christopher said, "Yes, I've seen what happened." He didn't want to be questioned about his statement, so he added, "On TV."

Colin told him how things got worse and worse. "My mum and dad were very concerned about the fighting. Most of it was in Belfast, but we weren't far away from that."

"So that's when you came here?"

"My dad was an American. The company offered him a promotion tied to a transfer to the States." Colin mentioned that the timing was just right. The transfer happened in the mid-1960s; the Northern Ireland – British conflict erupted into violence in the late 60s. "I didn't want to leave Ireland, but as it turned out, leaving Caryduff changed my life in many ways."

Christopher said, "What ways, Colin?"

Colin told him about standing in line at customs at the airport. When he looked around at all the people, his eyes became riveted on a pair of red shoes, worn by a young girl standing in a line next to his line. "I thought she was Dorothy from that movie."

Christopher laughed. "Did she click her heels?"

Colin laughed. "No, but my heart stopped when I looked at her. She was a very pretty lass. Very pretty indeed. We looked at each other and smiled. I wanted to go over to her, but I felt awkward. After the Customs Agent stamped our passports, I looked back at that pretty lass with the red shoes. Somehow, I knew I would see her again. Do you believe in destiny, Christopher?"

"Very much so." Christopher looked at his watch, waved to the waitress, and told Colin that he needed to get back to Goodwill. "How about breakfast tomorrow? Eight o'clock?" Colin nodded yes, they shook hands, and both left the restaurant.

———◦《◦》◦———

"Good morning. Glad we could get together again."

"I was looking forward to it, Christopher."

"That's very nice of you to say."

"There's a quote from that guy who made the Muppets. *'There's not a word yet for old friends who've just met.'* I feel like we're old friends. I hope you don't mind."

"I feel the same way, Colin."

"So, where were we? Oh, yeah. I landed in New York and we went to a hotel." He recalled being taken aback by the sight of tall buildings, the congestion on the roadways, and the noise of cars and trucks and horns. "When you leave a town of seven-thousand people and come to a town of seven-million, it's a bit intimidating."

Colin told Christopher about the family's apartment and adjusting to school. A week after they were situated, Colin registered at the local high school. "I was at my locker in the hallway, jiggling the combination lock. I dropped one of my books, and when I bent down to get it, a pair of red shoes appeared next to it."

For the next fifteen minutes Colin talked, non-stop, about his relationship with Clara – during high school, during the war, and very much during their life together after they married. "We were going to get married right after high school, but I was drafted into the Army. I served for two years, some of that time in Vietnam." Colin took the key ring out of his pocket, and kissed Clara's ring. "Clara kept me alive during the war. All I could think about when I was fighting, was wanting to be with my Clara."

"I noticed you have a slight limp when you walk."

"Shot in the foot, I was." Near the end of his tour in Vietnam, Colin became a Purple Heart recipient, and retired from military service. "And there's that destiny thing again. A bullet in my boot. Not my chest or head, but in my boot." Soon after Colin left the Army, he and Clara got married.

Needing a job, Colin perused the newspapers and canvassed his neighborhood looking for job openings. He happened on a shoe repair shop that just opened in a new strip mall. "My first thought was to get Clara's red shoes fixed. She broke the heel. I went in to ask how much it might cost, and struck-up a conversation with Bruno, the owner. We kind of got along. Well, guess what?"

"Hmm. He offered you a job?"

"I became an apprentice to Bruno, a middle-aged Italian immigrant who was full of piss and vinegar, and had the kindest heart of anyone I ever met – excluding, of course, my mother and Clara. He worked me hard, and taught me well. It's funny how you fall into things you don't expect. I never thought I'd become a cobbler, but there I was. I loved my work."

Christopher listened as Colin explained how he came to own the shop. "Bruno decided to retire. He offered to sell his business to me and I accepted. Things were going along just fine for many years, but like everything, things changed. The strip mall was, well, starting to look like crap. More people were buying new shoes rather than having their shoes fixed. My lease payments kept going up, and my income kept going down." Colin paused. He looked sullen. He bowed his head and tried to catch his breath before he cried. "Then, ten years ago…Clara and my son were killed in a car accident."

Seeing his face redden, and tears filling his eyes, Christopher reached out and placed his hand on Colin's. His touch was more comforting than any words he could say. Colin looked up and said, "Thank you." He took a big breath, and said, "I'm sorry for bending your ear."

"My ear is not bent," said Christopher. "In fact, I'm all ears, and my ears very much like hearing what you've been saying."

"That's what old friends say." Both of them smiled.

Christopher decided it was time to dive into his plan for Colin. "I only have a few minutes before I must leave. Could you tell me what your plan is? What do you want to do tomorrow, and the day after that?"

"Retire, I guess. Sell my machines, close shop, take it a day at a time. I lost my loving wife and son. I am going to lose my business. There's nothing left for me."

"You were passionate about being a cobbler. A great cobbler. If you walk away from your passion, you will eradicate happiness."

In an attempt to dodge Christopher's truthful statement, Colin replied, "Did the Muppet guy say that?"

Christopher chose to not answer, but did say, "I have an idea I'd like to share with you. Can we meet again tomorrow? Same time? Right here?"

———————

Colin walked into the restaurant a bit early and saw Christopher sitting in a booth with a guy dressed like a soldier. He waved and headed towards them. "Hi, Christopher."

"Hello again, Colin. Allow me to introduce you to Colonel Alan Bradford."

The Colonel stood, extended his hand, and said, "Happy to meet you, Colin." Colin extended his hand, but then decided to salute. "You're not in the army any more, Colin. Handshakes are perfectly fine." The three guys took their seats, called the waitress over, and placed their orders for breakfast.

"Christopher told me a little bit about your story. People like me tend to check people out. You know what I mean, I hope."

Colin told him that he understood why people who work for the government need to do that sometimes. "I hope you didn't find that I didn't pay for a parking ticket one time."

After a little bit of laughing, the Colonel became serious. "No, no parking tickets. In fact, you came up looking pretty darn good. Thank you for your service to our country."

"And thank you for *your* service, sir."

The Colonel told Colin about a U.S. Army base in upstate New York. "When you add the soldiers, families, and civilians together, there are more than 10,000 people there. We are pretty much self-sufficient. That is, we have just about everything we need, just like a small town. Just like Caryduff."

Colin nodded. and told the Colonel he knew about it. "I was never up that way, but I've heard it's a pretty nice base."

"Yes, it is. Well, when I said we have just about everything, one of the things we don't have is a shoe repair shop."

Colin sat up, his posture rigid. He knew exactly what the Colonel was getting at. "I'm sorry, sir, but as much as I want to serve America, I have to take a pass about reenlisting. I'm just too old anyway."

The Colonel explained that Colin did not have to re-enlist; he would be a civilian, working for the government without pay. "We'll set-up a shop for you on the base. It will cost you half of what your rent is now."

"You know how much I pay for rent? Wait, you're the government. Of course you know."

Without confirming or denying what he knew, the Colonel continued with his offer. "We'll give you a place to live that will cost less than half of what you're paying for your two-bedroom apartment."

"Two bedrooms, a kitchen, a living room, and as the folks at your base say, a latrine."

"Right. You will be able to shop in our commissary and eat in our chow hall."

"Do you have a Starbucks there? An Irish pub?"

Continuing to be dead serious, yet friendly, the Colonel said, "All we ask is that you charge a fair price for your labor. We're talking about at least 10,000 pairs of shoes and boots."

Christopher chimed in. "What do you think, Colin?"

Colin was not one to make rash decisions. "That's a lot of shoes and boots." He sat quietly, thinking, and making facial gestures as he talked to himself. Christopher's words about his passion danced in his mind. His only happiness in life for the last ten years was his cobbling.

"Well, Christopher, my old friend that I just met. Yesterday you asked me what I'm going to do tomorrow, and I now have an answer. Pack my bags, hammer, and awl. When do I start, Colonel?"

Christopher glanced up to the heavens, and under the table gave two thumbs up.

Capezio

When she said, "See you later, Harry," she felt tears starting to fill her eyes. "I'm going to Benny's. It's Monday, you know. Then to Goodwill. I should be back around three." She gently stroked the framed photograph on her dresser, and then left her apartment. She loved looking at their wedding picture. A handsome man in a tuxedo and a beautiful woman in a beautiful white gown. The photo didn't age while it sat on the dresser for the last 49 years, but Dolores did. Harry also aged till he died five years ago, but her memory of their wonderful life together didn't.

Ten minutes and three blocks later she arrived at five in the morning to help prep Benny's Diner for the breakfast crowd.

It was a typical weekday. Lots of the steadies came in and typically ordered the same thing. Pancakes, for reasons she never understood, seemed to be a favorite, especially for the construction workers. Many of the cops had black coffee and a donut. She didn't understand that either. Nor did she understand why Jewish guys thought they would die if they didn't have a bagel with cream cheese, and ordered it with Jewish jargon: *"A bagel with a schmear, Dolores."*

"You're looking especially beautiful this morning, Dolores," said Hank, an almost everyday customer.

In the four years she worked at Benny's she must have seen Hank a million times – well, maybe not quite that many times – and never figured out if he was Irish, Italian, Greek, or a mixed breed of some kind. When she asked him what his nationality was, he would reply "Brooklynese." The only things she was sure about were that Hank was a nice guy, probably single, and wanted to be more than a customer to Dolores.

Dolores poured coffee into Hank's cup as she looked at him with a smile on her face. "Now go on, Hank. Ain't nothin' beautiful about me, but it's nice to hear anyway."

"No, really, Dolores, you look terrific. If all women your age looked as good as you, the world would be filled with beautiful women."

Dolores was not offended by Hank's reference to her age. She felt that she actually did look pretty darn good for a 70-year-old. She felt herself blushing. She liked what she heard, but didn't want to agree with Hank because she thought vanity was not an admirable characteristic. "And if all men dished out the malarkey you're dishing out, there would be no difference between what's true and what's false."

Just then an elderly gentleman got up from his counter stool, pulled out money from his wallet, laid it on the counter, waved goodbye to Dolores and said, "Have a good day, honey." When Dolores took the money off the counter, she noticed it was a $20 bill. She blurted out, "Charlie, wait. You left me too much money.""

"Huh?"

"Your bill was $3.98. You left me a 20."

"I did?"

"Yup. I know I'm a great waitress, but a $16 tip is a bit over the top."

"You're a doll, Dolores. Thanks. Why don't you keep it anyway? There's a $1 tip for serving me breakfast, and a $15 tip for your honesty."

"It's too much, Charlie. Here's $15."

"Dolores, I'm a very old man, and also a very wise man. I know better than to argue with a woman. Okay, we'll split it. I'll take $10 from you and you keep the $5." He lowered his head slightly and stared at her with a grim look. "Do an old guy a favor and agree with me. I haven't had a woman agree with me for the...well, I don't know how many years."

"Okay, Charlie. Deal." She handed him a $10 bill and caressingly touched his cheek. "You have a good day, my friend."

Her day at the diner crept along for the next six hours. Looking up at the clock on the wall, and seeing that it was eleven, she anxiously waited for Mary to arrive to handle the lunch crowd. If Mary didn't arrive on time, Benny would have to convince Dolores to work a second shift. Her feet hurt from being on them for the last six hours. She didn't want to work another six, and she didn't want to hear Benny telling her that. She once witnessed his ways of convincing a waitress to work past her shift. Without an inkling of understanding or sorrow, he told her, "You gotta stay to help out, but if you can't, well, I can't see that you're going to get a paycheck next week."

The clock read five past eleven. Dolores saw Benny walking towards her. He called out, "Hey, Dolores."

Right behind Benny, Mary walked in. "Sorry, Benny. Had to take my kid to a neighbor 'cause my mother's sick and she couldn't..."

Benny cut her off. "Right. The kid. All I hear about from you is *the kid, the kid.*"

Wanting to calm the situation, Dolores purposely walked between Benny and Mary as she removed her apron and said, "See you tomorrow, Benny. By the way, is that a brand-new shirt? You look very good in it." Dolores had mixed feelings about Benny. He was gruff, demanding, and seemingly uncaring about how he treated people. On the other hand, she knew everyone had good inside of them. She reckoned that Benny's good side took a back seat as he drove himself to run a business so he could properly support his wife and two children. She once met his wife and kids and it was clear that Benny loved them.

As she strolled out of the diner she uttered "Yikes, my feet. Hey feet, take me to Goodwill and I'll take care of you." Fifteen minutes later she entered Goodwill and headed straight for where women's shoes were displayed. In less than a minute she found the casual shoes that looked to be in good condition and were her size. "Here we go, feet. Let's see if you like them." She kicked off her old shoes that were in terrible need of repair, and slipped on the new ones. "They're used shoes, feet, but new to you."

When she got up from the chair and walked around, two things happened. First was that her feet felt great. The shoes not only fit, they were comfortable and looked good. She smiled. "Okay feet. I gave you a present, now give me one and let me walk home without any pain."

Second, a sparkle of light on the tip of a black shoe caught her eye. It was as if the shoe was saying "Hey, look at me." She walked over to the shoe. It was a pair of low-heeled dress shoes. She looked at them, touched them, but then decided it was silly to think she should buy them. *When will I ever have the need to wear a pair of shoes like this?* She thought.

"Nice shoes, aren't they, Dolores?" said Christopher, a Goodwill employee.

"Yes, they're nice. Do I know you? How do you know my name?"

"You work at Benny's Diner, don't you?" Christopher was never at Benny's and he never met Dolores before. His question was not a lie. He wasn't allowed to lie.

Dolores, however, took the question as a statement. She assumed that he saw her name on her apron.

"Yes, I do. I guess you saw me there. Are you a pancake or bagel and schmear guy?"

"Ah, I'm more of a bacon and eggs guy. Nice shoes, aren't they?"

"Yes, but I don't need them."

"They're dancing shoes, you know."

"Dancing shoes?"

"They're meant for dancing. The soles are suede so you can glide on the dance floor, and the heels, they're called Spanish heels, are very strong. They won't break off."

"Dancing? I haven't danced for the last ten years. I lost my husband five years ago. For the five years before that he was quite ill."

Christopher knew all of that, but certainly could not let on that he did. "I'm sorry to hear that. I hope he is happy in heaven."

"Me too."

"Why don't you try these on, just for kicks? Sorry, no pun intended."

Dolores smiled. She liked the pun. "How much are they?"

"They're very expensive. They were made by Capezio, a world renowned dance shoe maker. I wouldn't be surprised if Ginger Rogers had several pairs of Capezios." Christopher didn't know if Ginger Rogers had any Capezios, and he knew that his statement, verbatim, was not a lie. "However, they're used. Let's say slightly used, but in very good condition. They're $5."

Dolores decided to put them on. While Christopher stood by, she sat down, slipped off her about-to-be-purchased casual shoes, and put on the dancing shoes. She got up and walked around. Her walk turned into a rhythmic prancing. She wanted to dance. "Whew, these shoes must have some magic in them. I feel like I want to dance again."

"I think Capezio made them especially for you."

"$5?"

"Yes."

She sat down, took off the dancing shoes and put on her casual shoes. She had a strange feeling that Charlie gave her an extra $5 tip just so she could buy the dance shoes. "Kismet, Christopher. I just happen to have an extra $5, so I'll buy them?"

———⸺《◉》⸺———

Friday night came. With her work week over, Dolores did what she and Harry usually did on Friday nights. She put the packaged pizza in the oven, turned on the gas, and turned on the TV to watch an old movie. TCM was about to play "Shall We Dance," starring

Fred Astaire and Ginger Rogers. "Kismet again," she said. She went to her closet and took out the Capezios. "You gotta dress the part to really get into a movie," she said. The oven timer dinged.

Sitting on the sofa in front of the TV, she ate the pizza and was mesmerized by the dance routines in the movie. She didn't have restless legs syndrome, so she assumed that her feet must have been listening to the music and tapped the floor and then slid around. A phone call interrupted her dancing feet. "Hello?"

"Dolores, it's Sylvia. I hope you didn't forget about the birthday party tomorrow at St. Agnes."

"Oh, I don't know Sylvia. I think I just want to stay home and rest."

Sounding stern, yet compassionate, Sylvia said, "Dolores, now listen to me. You've been alone for a long time, and it's now time to not be alone. You need to socialize. You need to do more than work, clean, and watch TV alone. Harry would want you to be out with people and living life."

"I miss him, Sylvia."

"I know, honey. I know. But life for you has to go on."

There was a long pause. Sylvia knew Dolores was taking her words to heart, and hoping that she would agree to go to the party. She then heard Dolores sigh. "Okay, I'll be there tomorrow."

———◉———

The hall in the basement of the church was filled with Happy Birthday balloons and streamers. Everyone wore silly conical party hats made of thin cardboard. Dolores guessed that there were nearly a hundred people there. Although surrounded by the people who were milling around, talking, laughing, drinking, and eating, Dolores felt alone. What little desire she had to be one of the crowd, to participate in the festivities, was overshadowed by her desire to be with Harry.

"Hello. I'm Enrico Abrezio," said a handsome man who stood before her with his hand extended, signaling a handshake.

"Abrezio? Did you say Abrezio?"

"Yes, Abrezio. But please call me Enrico."

"Do you know Capezio?"

"No, but I'm sure you could teach me that dance. Would you like to?"

There was something about Enrico that drew her closer to him. He was about the same age as Harry would have been had he lived. He was a head taller than she was, about the same height as Harry. He had silver hair. So did Harry. The connections stopped there. He didn't look anything like Harry, and he clearly spoke with a slight foreign accent. Harry didn't. With a tender smile, she said, "Sorry that I confused you. Capezio isn't a dance. It's the name of a shoe."

With a quizzical expression he said, "Hmm. A shoe. And what is your name?"

"I'm Dolores. Yes."

"Yes? Is that your last name?"

With an almost giggle she said, "No. My last name isn't yes. Yes, I would like to dance."

They danced a slow waltz. They drank punch and ate some birthday cake. They danced a foxtrot, then a Charleston. They talked. They laughed. Dolores had no pain in her feet, or in her heart. For the first time in a long time, Dolores was not alone.

In the back room, out of sight from Dolores and Enrico, Christopher looked up and said, "Did I do okay?"

E ric's fingers glided over the bumps and across the smooth valleys. His eyes, opened wide as if he was experiencing a miracle, moved from left to right, up and down. When he closed his eyes, he could feel the warmth of the reds and coolness of the blues. He felt an emotional shiver. His thoughts raced. *How does someone do that? How do they know what colors to use? Why did they give it to Goodwill?*

Christopher approached and stood next to Eric and joined him in staring at the painting. "Hi. Really nice painting, isn't it?"

Eric turned his head and looked at Christopher.

"Christ?"

"Pardon."

Eric pointed to Christopher's shirt. His name was sewn on the breast pocket of his Goodwill employee shirt. A cleaning towel was strung across his shoulder that covered the *opher*. Christopher smiled when he realized what Eric saw. He removed the towel and said, "Oh, I see. It's Christopher. "

"Yup, a really nice painting." He looked at his watch which read six o'clock, and said, "Gotta go. Job's awaitin'. See ya."

Christopher nodded. "Yup, I will be seeing you."

"Huh?"

"I mean, I hope to see you again. Take care."

Eric left the store, hopped on the bike that he bought at Goodwill months ago, and sped off to his second job as part of the cleaning crew at Madison High School. He peddled as fast as he could, his body bent in a racing position. He forcefully squeezed the handles on the handlebar to the point that blood couldn't flow into them. He wasn't late for work; he was letting out the anger that lived in him and gnawed at his soul.

⚊⚊⚊◆⚊⚊⚊

After a lonely late night in his small apartment, he awakened when the sun peered through the iron fire escape and lit his bedroom. He poured hot water into the cup and then mixed a spoonful of instant coffee into it. He took a sip and muttered, "The breakfast of champions!"

He sat on one of the two chairs in the kitchen part of his living room. No one ever sat on the other chair. He looked out the window while he drank. Trucks with roaring engines passed by. Cars ran stop signs and red traffic lights. Not too many kids played on sidewalks because the drug dealers didn't like having them around. Not too many people walked through the neighborhood for pleasure. Not too many people liked where they lived, and that included Eric. But that's all he could afford.

He often mused about what life would be if his parents didn't die in that car crash when he was ten years old. He wondered if he would have been in a different place, a better spot, if they had any relatives that would have adopted him. There were none. He became a foster child. He lived on and off in a state facility, and with three different foster parents during his eight years in the system. He looked back at those times and remembered the good and the bad. The good was that he was physically cared for with food, clothing, and if needed, medicine; the bad was that none of the foster parents nourished his soul or taught him how to confront life. He didn't feel loved, and he didn't feel love for others. His mind was filled with anger; his heart was empty.

When he turned 18, he left foster care. The money he received from the state allowed him to become self-sufficient, for a while. He had enough money to rent his apartment for a few months, pay for his utilities, and put food on the table. He needed to get a job. Lacking vocational skills, the only doors that were open to him paid very little. Having two jobs was the only answer. That landed him at Bert's Car Wash. His buddy at Bert's gave him the lead to join the high school cleaning crew.

He placed the empty coffee cup in the sink and strolled out, double locking the door behind him. He muttered again, "Another day, another dollar." His thought was, *whoever said that must have had the same jobs I have.*

"Yo, Bert. Where am I today?

"You're *out.*"

"You got it. But hey, Bert, I don't want to complain, but it seems I haven't done *in* in a long time."

"I agree, Eric. You shouldn't complain. There's a batch of rags in the dryer. See you later."

Eric was rightfully upset. When he got the job at Bert's he was told he would be rotated between the greeters and the wipe down folks, which everyone called the *in* and *out* jobs. The rotation was not fair. Eric knew Bert favored some workers, and more often than not, gave them the easier *in* jobs. He learned from his various foster parents to not complain about anything; to be grateful that he had a place to live and be fed. He learned that he had to keep anger in, not express it lest he be kicked back into a state facility. He believed that the *Keep your mouth shut and be thankful with what you have* rule also applied to his job. It ate at him.

With the sun starting its plunge to the other side of Earth, the car wash closed for the day. Eric clocked out of Bert's, and raced on his bike to Goodwill.

———◦((◦))◦———

"Hello again. It's Eric, right?"

With a smile Eric said, "Yeah, and I'm glad to see your whole name."

"Still looking at the paintings?"

"Yeah, but the one I really liked is gone. Somebody buy it?"

"That's what usually happens. At least, that's what Goodwill hopes happens." Christopher pulled a painting out of his cart. "I was just about to hang this one up. Want to see it?"

"Sure." Eric looked at it and liked the scene. It was a seascape, a sunset over the ocean as seen from a deserted beach. He ran his fingers across the water and beach. There were no bumps or valleys, but he was fascinated by what he thought the painter would want him to feel. "This one's flat. The other one wasn't."

"The other one was painted with oil paints. This one

was painted with acrylic paint. Different paints, different results. But art, as they say, is in the eyes of the beholder. In your case, art is also in the fingertips of the beholder. You might see beauty in a painting while others don't. You might touch a painting and it touches your soul."

"I wish I could afford to buy some of these."

"I'm sure someday you will be able to. But did you ever consider creating your own painting?"

"Nah. I can't do that. The closest I ever got to making a picture was when I was maybe five or six. I had some crayons. Didn't turn out that good so I tore it up."

"Did you know that Michelangelo destroyed many of his paintings and drawings?"

"You're kiddin'. He did? Why?"

"Oh, the *why* isn't important. The fact that he did is what matters. I can't think of anyone, any famous artist, who has not burned, tore up, or somehow destroyed some of his or her art." Christopher cleared his throat and raised his eyes upward as he thought, *That's not a lie. At this moment I can't think of anyone who has not.*

"Whoops. Gotta go. My mop is calling me. Adios."

Eric returned to Goodwill the next day. The tip jar at the car wash was filled more than it usually was, and his share of the tips was therefore more than he usually got. He thought *Extra cash. I'm going to buy that flat painting.*

When he arrived at Goodwill the painting was gone. Christopher happened to be in the area carrying a cardboard box. "Christopher! It's gone. Man, you guys sell stuff pretty quick."

"Yes, sometimes we do, sometimes we don't. Take this box of stuff, for example. It's been on the floor for over a week. No one wants it."

"What's in it?"

"Tubes of paint, paint brushes, and other stuff that painters use. Want to buy it? It's half price Wednesday."

"Nah, I don't think so. But I could use a pair of shoes. See you later."

At the shoe rack Eric glanced at the various shoes and boots and slippers. He was attracted to one pair because it looked a little bit like a painting. Paint was splattered on both shoes. Christopher put the box of paints and brushes in the back room so no one else would buy it. He then meandered over to the shoe rack. "Interesting shoes, aren't they?" he asked Eric.

"Yeah. It's like they were made that way, not from an accident when someone spilled paint on them."

Christopher cleared his throat, pointed at the paint shoes, and then at Eric's feet.

Eric understood his sign language. "Sure, why not?" He slipped into the paint shoes and immediately felt relaxed. It was like the feeling he sometimes had when he took a hot shower and just stood there, wearing the warmth of the water as it rained on his body. He looked at the price tag that read $10. "Half price on these too?"

"Yes, half price."

He was laughing and prancing around. "Eric's got a new pair of shoes! A new pair of used shoes. I do, I do, I do."

"I wonder, Eric. Maybe it's a coincidence. I don't know. But you wanted to buy a painting and you bought a pair of shoes that you thought looked like a painting. And then I happened to be carrying a box full of painting stuff."

"Yeah, it's gotta be a coincidence. It's not like God or some magician put all that together at the same time just for me."

"What if it was like that? Do you know what destiny is?"

"Yeah, I know." His voice slowly got louder as he spoke. He was no longer calm. "My destiny already happened. A black kid whose mom and dad died and I was destined to be raised by the state and foster parents who were more interested in making some damn money than taking care of me. And then I'm on my own and work at cleaning shit-stained toilet bowls and wiping down cars and saying thank you even if I didn't get a tip. And I wonder what's going to happen the next day *if* the next day happens."

Christopher heard and felt the anger that Eric carried. He sounded lost and in need of a friend. "Eric, it's none of my business. But I've been around a lot longer than you, like a couple of hundred years longer than you."

"Only two hundred?"

"Yes, that is humorous. If you can take an old guy's advice, you should think about your destiny. Not what happened in the past. You can't change that. Think about what might happen, what could happen, in the future. And think about what you can do to make sure it's the destiny you want."

Eric became sullen. He felt uneasy when his anger erupted, but letting it out, hearing himself saying what he did, calmed him. He wanted to cry. He wanted to run. He wanted to rest. "I need to sit down. Maybe it's the shoes that made me a little dizzy."

"Sure, right here. I'll be back in a minute." Christopher went to the back room where he had placed the box of painting supplies. He returned to Eric who had just gotten up from the chair. "Eric, no one is going to buy this stuff, so I bought it. I haven't given anyone a present in a very long time, but I'd like to give it to you. Please take it."

Eric did take it. He filled his backpack with all the paint and brushes, shook Christopher's hand with both of his hands, looked squarely into Christopher's eyes and said, "You're a good guy, like an angel maybe. Thank you." Eric left to go to Madison High.

———※(()》※———

He hadn't worn his paint shoes for a couple of days, but when Sunday arrived – his day off from both jobs – he put them on. He sat in the kitchen drinking his instant coffee. He looked at the stack of paint tubes and brushes piled in the corner. He thought *What the hell? I'll give it a try.* He didn't have any canvases to paint on, so he thought he'd go to Goodwill and see if he could buy one cheaply. Just then lightning struck.

Dark clouds filled the sky. Rain drops splattered loudly on his kitchen window, sounding more like pebbles than water hitting the glass. A lightning bolt lit the sky. The bang of thunder sounded like the world was exploding. He noticed something he never noticed before. The wall around the kitchen window had several long cracks in it. Another lightning bolt crackled. His mind connected the bolt to the crack. "Wow, my wall is the sky and storm. Ha!"

Wanting to capture the thought he had about the bolt and the crack, he opened several tubes of paint. He used his kitchen table as a palette, squeezing tubes of black, white, red, yellow, and blue onto it. Each color made a small mound that he thought looked like mini-mountains. He also made mini-mountains with some paints he never knew had names, like raw umber, dioxazine purple, and quinacridone magenta. He spent the next five hours, uninterrupted, save making another cup of coffee, painting a mural on the kitchen wall. Once finished, he stepped back and looked at his creation. It was a skyscape of his neighborhood during a storm. He painted a dark sky and a lightning bolt. He painted people alone in their apartments looking out their window, fearing the storm. He painted people running down the street, hunched over thinking that they would avoid getting wet if they ran that way. The mural exuded darkness, danger, and loneliness.

<hr>

The weeks passed quickly as Eric kept very busy with his two jobs, and now his third job: painting. He scrounged around the neighborhood looking for things to paint on. Large pieces of wood, bricks, and slabs of sheetrock found at a construction site served him well. He found a bucket filled with tubes of paint at a yard sale and bought the whole bucket. He worked hard at Madison and at Bert's, and even harder at painting. His passion for painting allowed him to feel that he had a purpose in life.

———•(•)•———

"Hi Christopher."

"Eric. Good to see you."

"You gave me a present once. It's now my turn. Here's a present for you." Eric handed him his latest painting, painted on a piece of canvas that he nailed to a piece of wood that used to be part of a desk that someone tossed into the street.

"It's beautiful, Eric. Thank you. Have you been painting a lot?"

"Yes. My apartment is filled with lots of paintings. I'm running out of walls to hang them on."

"Why don't you try to sell them?"

"How? Where?"

"Why not in your apartment? Think of it as an art gallery. Invite people to come by. I'll help you do that."

———•(•)•———

A couple of weeks later many people came to what he called *Eric's Art Gallery*. One of them, Charles Ingle, invited by Christopher, was the owner of Ingalls Art Gallery. Ingalls was astounded by what he saw. "Eric, you're a talented guy. I'd like to buy some of your works. I wish I could also buy your wall. Wow!! One helluva mural!"

A couple of months later Eric's art was featured at Ingalls. His paintings were arranged by date, from the earliest to the most recent. Even a casual observer could see the evolution of Eric's thoughts about life. Subject matter and colors transitioned from being dark and full of despair, to brilliant light and hopefulness. Every one of his paintings sold. Each one put more money in Eric's pocket than two months' salary from his two jobs. One buyer wanted to buy Eric's kitchen table if he signed it. It was on display under the framed *About the Artist* hanging on the wall.

Christopher was in attendance at the Ingalls exhibit. He sipped the champagne that was served, raised his glass and toasted Eric from afar. He then looked up, raised his glass, and made another toast.

A s he walked past Cameron, he caustically said, "Get a job!"

"I have one, mister. This one. I really need a couple of bucks to make a better sign." Cameron encountered many people like that guy. Some said nasty things; most simply ignored him; a few dropped some money in his empty Folgers coffee can.

"You should give him some money. That was a funny line about needing a new sign," said his wife.

"No damn way. There's no reason why he has to beg. He can get a job. He can take a shower. He can get rid of that awful smell that's ruining my appetite." His wife decided to not pursue that conversation. Too often when they disagreed her irascible husband would ruin her day.

Right behind the couple was Christopher, stopping in at Applebee's for lunch during his break from Goodwill. He did not judge them. He knew they had their reasons for being the way they are, just like all people have their reasons for being who they are, and how they live their lives. Cameron included. Christopher dropped $1 in the jar, and said, "This is for making me laugh with what you said to that gentleman. God bless you."

"And God bless you, my friend."

Sitting at the counter he was within ear-shot of the

guy he saw outside who was arguing with his wife. Christopher was not one to eavesdrop, but couldn't turn his ears off to the loud voices. "Betsy, do you mind if I move down to the end of the counter. For some reason this seat is just not comfortable."

"Sure, Christopher."

When he finished his lunch, he ordered a *very hot coffee* to go. "And can you please give me one of those cream packets, a few sugar packets, and a stirrer?"

He carried his to-go order to Cameron and handed it to him. "I thought this might warm your bones a little bit."

Cameron stood up from his squatting position, looked at Christopher with a grateful expression, and took the coffee and packets from him. "Some people are...I don't want to curse...well, they're just jerks. And some are angels. I'm pretty darn sure you're an angel."

Christopher smiled and whispered, "You're right. I really am an angel. Please don't tell anyone." Both of them laughed. Christopher said he had to get back to work. "You take care, son." Cameron looked at Christopher as he walked away. His hand was warm from holding the hot coffee, and his heart also seemed to warm up.

———————— ((◉)) ————————

A week later Christopher noticed that Cameron was sitting outside of Goodwill. The store was about to open. He parked in the employee section of the parking lot, and entered Goodwill through the back door. A half-hour later the manager unlocked the front door and Cameron walked in. "Can I help you, sir?" asked the manager.

Cameron replied, "I have this need to go on a spending spree and thought Goodwill was just the place to be."

Noticing Cameron's slightly torn and dirty clothing, a beard that should have been trimmed years ago and shampooed last night, the manager surmised that all Cameron wanted was to get warm on that almost freezing day. The manager cleared his throat and calmly said, "I'm sorry sir. Please leave." Cameron looked forlorn. His lips quivered as if he was about to say something, but decided that the manager had every right to tell him to leave. Had he argued, had he decided to fight his way into the store, he knew the consequences would have been much greater than simply having to go outside into the cold.

"Hi there," said Christopher as he walked to the front door. I'm glad you made it." He grabbed Cameron's arm and escorted him to the donation area at the back of the store. The manager scrunched his face, giving Christopher a *what's that all about?* look. Christopher signaled back by nodding and raising his hand signifying *don't you worry about it.*

"I think I should introduce myself. I'm Christopher, and as you probably figured out, I work here."

Cameron was delighted that he was in the warm store, yet confused as to why Christopher gave him passage. "Uh, I'm Cameron. You can call me Cam if you want."

"I'll call you Cameron." Christopher went over to the kitchenette and poured some coffee into two cups. "I just made this. Hope you like it. Want some cream? Some sugar?"

"Black is great. Thanks."

"Tell me about yourself, Cameron."

Between small sips of the very hot coffee, Cameron said, "Not much to tell. I'm a homeless bum scrounging for nickels and dimes so I can survive."

"*Survive* is an interesting word, but it doesn't have the same meaning as *live.*"

"Yeah, well, I'm alive. I guess. And I have my good days, like right now. Warm. Hot coffee. Talking to a nice guy."

The manager approached them. With sarcasm apparent, he said, "Christopher, I'm terribly sorry for breaking up this wonderful party you're having, but customers are coming into the store."

Christopher put his coffee mug into the sink. Cameron followed suit. They shook hands. "Thanks again. Ain't many people out there like you." Cameron departed. Christopher went to work, to what he considered his secondary job, that of sorting and pricing donations, and helping customers find what they were looking for.

———— ((●)) ————

At Christopher's suggestion, Cameron visited Goodwill just about every day to have hot coffee in a warm room. Their conversations were pleasant, and always superficial. They talked about old movies, the traffic jams on nearby streets, and various other inconsequential topics.

The day before Thanksgiving Day, Cameron sat on a recliner while chatting with Christopher. "There's a hole in your soul, Cameron."

Cameron bent his leg and crossed it over his other leg, looking at the sole of his considerably scuffed shoes. "Yup, big hole alright. Gotta put some more cardboard in there."

"Well, hold on there. We got a donation yesterday with a lot of men's shoes." Christopher pulled out several pairs from the bin. "This pair looks pretty good, and I'm guessing it's your size."

Cameron slipped then on. A perfect fit. He walked around looking down at his shoes. Not only did they look good and feel comfortable, he had the strange sensation of feeling more alive. "I like 'em. And no hole in the sole. How much are they?"

"Let's just say they're a Thanksgiving present from Goodwill."

"Okie dokie. Thanks. And Happy Thanksgiving to you."

The front door opened for customers. Cameron pranced out the back door. Christopher got to sorting and pricing.

———⋙《◉》⋘———

"Good morning. You're here earlier than usual. Everything okay?"

"Couldn't be better. Well, of course it could be better, but right now it feels pretty good to me."

"Why's that, Cameron?"

Cameron sat down on a donated bar stool, took a sip of coffee, and said, "I didn't have a nightmare last night."

"Oh, do you usually have them?"

"Had one every night for the last...I don't know how many years."

"I'm sorry to hear that. Do you have any idea why?"

Cameron looked more relaxed than usual. He spoke with less anxiety in his tone. "I think it was the war. No, it was definitely the war." He paused. His body slumped. His wrist became limp. He almost spilled his coffee. With a slight shudder in his voice he said, "I killed people. Faceless people that I didn't know. I see them in my nightmares, bloodied, dying, crying out."

Christopher was fully aware of how Cameron felt, and understood the PTSD that hit him. He suffered the same disorder when he fought in the Civil War, but it was called *nostalgia* back then. "Cameron, listen to me. You fought in a war to protect our freedom. This is the land of the free. You, my friend, were part of the brave that allows us to be free."

Cameron's calm disappeared. His slumped body became rigid as he sat higher in his chair. He slammed his mug on the table; his hands became fists. Anger filled his face. With a loud voice he said, "Christ! Don't you get it? I murdered people. I see them. I see my bullet smashing into their head, their gun flying in the air as they fall back and blood squirting from their brain."

Christopher was always unflappable. He knew that Cameron needed to scream out. He needed to relive the events and hear himself. He needed to connect with the events – not in a dream, but consciously. Moments passed. Cameron calmed down as his tears swelled. He cleared his throat and rubbed his arm across his eyes. "I'm sorry. I shouldn't have gotten so angry. You don't deserve my anger. I'm okay now."

Christopher leaned into Cameron and said, "You're

not okay, but you can be. You need to face the situation squarely. You need to know how you were willing to give your life to save other lives. I know many people are thankful for what you did for them. You should be proud."

"Yeah, I know. I know."

"Would it have been better for you, for me, for any person in America if your enemy killed you?" Cameron couldn't answer that question just then. Too many thoughts were buzzing in his head; too many emotions were bombarding him. Christopher continued to talk to him.

He painted metaphors in Cameron's mind, speaking of life as a journey, as if it was a road trip. "You hit bumps and potholes. They're temporary obstacles and you get past them. Rain storms make the road slippery, and you drive more carefully, but sometimes you skid. You come to intersections and need to decide if you go straight or turn. If you make the wrong decision, you might get lost, but that is also temporary. You eventually find your way."

Cameron listened attentively, soaking up everything Christopher said. "My mind used to be focused, and then all my thoughts became a blur. Yeah, I lost my way. I lost my wife and son – he's twenty now and I haven't seen him for ten years. "

Looking at the wall clock, Christopher said, "Enough for now, Cameron. I need to get back to work. Think about what we just discussed, and please, let's continue talking." Cameron nodded in agreement, firmly shook Christopher's hand, and left.

Months rolled by. Winter ebbed, allowing trees and flowers to bloom. The seeds of understanding and introspection Christopher planted in Cameron's mind and heart took root.

Over dinner at Applebee's, Cameron told Christopher that he applied for the accounting job. "I think it went well. They'll let me know in a few days."

"Fabulous, Cameron. You not only look good on the outside with your new suit and clean-shaven face, I think you look pretty darn good on the inside."

Cameron mused on the problems he faced for the last ten years, and how *living* trumps *surviving*. "If not for you, Christopher…"

Christopher cut him off. "It's you, not me. If not for *you* taking the bull by the horns and facing realities, we wouldn't be here tonight eating too much food that's bound to make us fat." They laughed, they ate, and they talked about the future. "What's his name, Cameron?"

"Who?"

"Your son."

Cameron stopped eating. He pursed his lips and closed his eyes. Seconds passed. "Josh. His name is Josh."

"Where is Josh now?"

"I don't know."

"Where is his mother now?"

"I don't know."

"Where were they the last time that you saw them?"

Cameron knew exactly where Christopher was heading with his questions. "I can't. They don't know me anymore. I'm sure I'm dead to them."

"There was someone else that people thought had

died. They were the people that believed in him. They didn't stop believing in him after he died.

"Come on, Christopher, I'm not Jesus."

"No, you're not. You're Cameron. You're a good guy. You were a husband and a father. Your family believed in you. You were a soldier. You said you lost your way, but it seems you've gotten on the right road again. It's now up to you to move ahead, or turn off the road. You can't park your car and just sit in it."

———— ((●)) ————

Summer came. Cameron's new job was working out well. He liked all the people with whom he worked, and all the people liked him. He felt like he did a dozen years ago – energetic, focused, worthy. Only one thing could have made him happier.

"Have a good weekend, Cameron. Don't get hit by any firecrackers."

"I'm hoping I will. Have a good weekend, that is." Independence Day was a good name for how he felt. As he drove the 150 miles to the town he used to live in, he thought again about Christopher's road trip metaphors. He knew he made some wrong turns in the past, but none was on purpose. He understood the reasons for his journey in the last dozen years, and forgave himself for succumbing to the detours.

He stopped his car across the street from where he needed to go. Looking out the window he saw a young man mowing the lawn. He started to walk across the street, and then stopped. He thought, *I can't. What could I say? Was he told that I died?*

The young man also stopped. He turned the mower to idle to reduce the noise. He looked at the man in the middle of the street wondering why he was standing there. He thought, *A salesman? Someone who got lost and needed directions?* "Yo, can I help you?" Cameron gave a slight wave and continued to walk ahead. When he was about ten feet from the young man, he heard a question that filled his heart: "Dad?"

"**W**hen did you start bleeding, Gloria?" asked her Ob-Gyn.

"Last night. I went to pee and when I flushed, I saw the blood."

"You had a miscarriage, Gloria."

Gloria hoped his examination was as perfunctory as his statement. "Are you sure?"

"Yes. This is the third time in the last eighteen months. It's been taking a toll on your body. I'm sorry to say that a full-term pregnancy is probably not in the cards for you. And if you do get pregnant, giving birth could be very dangerous for you."

"Is there anything that can be done?"

"I recommend that you have a hysterectomy. On the bright side, you won't have to be concerned with menstrual cycles."

"Bright side? You have to be kidding!. Men have no idea how important it is to a woman to have a child. I'm outta here!"

Gloria left Dr. Mark Albright's office and wanted to kick every chair she passed in the waiting room. She pressed the key remote and her car *beep-beeped.* She made a fist, pointed her middle finger up, and screamed out, "Beep-beep to you!" Her anger found its way to her car door when she kicked it. Bending over the car's hood, she pounded it with her fists. "Damn it! Damn it!" she cried out. A passerby asked if she was okay. Gloria yelled at the woman, "Does it look like I'm okay? Leave me alone! Go get pregnant!"

She was ordinarily a cautious driver, but the anger she felt clouded her thinking. She backed out her car from her parking slot, not paying attention to what might be behind her. She didn't see the woman wheeling a baby carriage when she turned to exit. She was lucky that she happened to catch an image in her rear-view mirror. She slammed on the brakes the same time that the woman screamed.

The woman came up to her car window, just looking at her. She lowered her window and apologized, profusely. The woman said, "You didn't hit me or my baby, but you could have. Please drive more carefully." Gloria was astounded by what she said. *How can a person who was almost killed be so calm, so accepting?* Gloria stayed in the exit lane, pondering the woman's statement. *I could have hit her, yet she remained calm. She seemed to have cared about me.* She mumbled to herself, "Get hold of yourself. Grow up. Life will go on." She heard a horn honk, woke from her introspection, and exited.

———— ((•)) ————

Claude came home from work. Having said *hi* to Gloria, and not getting a response, he knew she was not in the best of moods. He kicked off his shoes, poured himself a scotch on the rocks, sat down next to her on the sofa, and said: "One of those days?"

Claude listened to Gloria as she talked about her day that was filled with depression, anger, and almost killing a woman and her baby. "Well, you didn't kill the woman or her baby, so that's a good thing."

"That's it, Claude? That's your take on my day?"

Claude sheepishly said, "No, no, no. It was the last thing you said so I thought I'd comment on what was good about it." Slightly intoxicated, Gloria didn't have the wherewithal to argue with him.

"So, what are you going to do about the hysterectomy?" he asked.

"I haven't made up my mind. I know you want a child. So do I. Dr. Shithead thinks I should forget about that. I don't know. What do you think I should do?"

Claude rose from the sofa and walked around the room with his hands in his pocket and head looking down. "I want a child, Gloria. It seems you can't have one. I don't know either."

Gloria was concerned about his tone. She always found Claude very decisive about everything. This was the first time he didn't say how he felt or what he wanted to do. "What if I decide to have a hysterectomy? Will we still be *us*?"

His reaction continued to bother her. He kept on walking around, looking down, not saying a word. He stopped walking and knelt in front of her. "You know I love you, don't you?" She nodded. "You know that I want to marry you, don't you?" She nodded again, but her eyes contained a question: *What is he going to say next?* "I need to think about it. I don't want to make a rash decision. I need time."

The conversation ebbed to silence. Neither talked. Gloria went to the bathroom. When he heard the bath water filling the tub, he gulped down the last of his scotch, went to the bedroom, disrobed, and went to bed.

When Gloria awakened in the morning, Claude was not in bed. The time on the dresser clock told her that he already left for work. She went about her typical morning routine of yoga, hygiene, and a light breakfast. As a volunteer at the local food bank, she wasn't compelled to go to work, but she didn't want to stay in the apartment alone. She needed the comfort of human interaction.

Spending time at the food bank was the perfect therapy. She heard stories from people who had far bigger problems than she had. It helped put her problem into perspective. She chatted with her friend, Beth, about her miscarriage. That helped her objectively consider her alternatives. When she returned home her resolve was absolute. She would tell Claude that she didn't want to have a baby whose mother might die while giving birth.

"Claude, are you home?" He wasn't. She poured half a glass of Chardonnay and relaxed on her sofa. It was then she saw a note on the coffee table. She felt it wasn't "Went to the grocery store for milk." She didn't want to read it, but had to.

The note read, "I am so sorry. I love you, and will always love you, but it is time to move on. Regardless of what you decide to do I will be faced with not having a child with you, or having a child that I might have to raise on my own. I cannot live with that. Claude"

She sat back. The note dropped on her lap. She bowed her head, staring at the note, but not really seeing it. A tear dropped from her eye, landing on Claude's name. The tear obliterated it.

Morning came. The sun streamed in through the window and lit her face awakening her from her night's sleep spent on the sofa. After her morning routine she scoured the apartment, and tossed reminders of Claude into the trash. Framed photos, memorabilia from several vacations they took, and any clothing he happened to forgot to take with him, were tossed. One box remained in the closet – on her side of the closet. It was marked "The Day."

She carefully picked up each item in the box, looking at it, and sometimes breathing in the odor. All of the items were collected for *The Day* she would give birth. Every item was unique; some were her favorites: A crib mobile she found in an antique store, baby clothing hand-sewn by her mother, and baby booties hand-crafted by a Navajo woman, and painted with the hummingbird symbol to signify the miracle of living. All went back into the box.

"Hello. A donation I assume?" asked Christopher.

"Yes. I hope all of it is put to good use," said Gloria.

Christopher opened the box to see the assortment of baby items. He didn't have to think hard to figure out why Gloria was donating the items to Goodwill. "Thank you. I'm sure everything will be put to good use for a needy family. Would you like a receipt?" Gloria nodded no, gave him a slight smile and drove off.

The day had ended for donation giving. Christopher closed and locked the drop-off area door and set about to sorting and pricing. He took the baby booties from the box, held them up to the sky, and whispered, "Yes, they will be put to good use."

———————

A week passed. Curious to see if the items she donated to Goodwill were purchased, she paid a visit to the store. Walking towards the area that was filled with baby and toddler items, she spied a woman with a baby carriage. She was startled. From the side it looked very much like the woman she almost ran over. *This is beyond coincidence,* she thought. She approached the woman and said, "Hi."

The woman turned to face Gloria. With a relatively loud voice, and looking nervous, she said, "What?"

Realizing that was not the woman she almost killed, she said, "Nothing. I was just saying 'hi,' you know?"

Still seeming nervous, the woman asked Gloria if she could watch her baby for a minute. "The ladies' room is too small to wheel this carriage inside."

"Sure. No problem." The woman walked away. Gloria looked down at the baby, guessing it was a girl. Much more than a minute passed. Gloria wheeled the carriage to the ladies' room and knocked on the door. "Are you okay, Miss?" There was no answer.

She opened the door to find no one there. She wheeled the carriage around the store frantically looking for the woman. She asked customers and employees to help find her. No one did. She was gone. The store manager called 911. Moments later the police arrived and took Gloria's testimony. They reviewed the surveillance video, but unfortunately only the back of the woman appeared on camera. Child Protective Services arrived. Gloria was told that the baby was in good hands and she could leave. She left. CPS asked Christopher if the stuff they found in the carriage belonged to Goodwill. Christopher said, "Take it all. It might be useful."

———※◀◉▶※———

"It was great having dinner with you. We really should do this more often."

"You're right, honey. See ya tomorrow at the food bank?" said Beth.

Gloria gave her a hug, waved goodbye, and said, "See ya." Walking a couple of blocks to where she parked her car, she noticed a scantily dressed woman on a street corner. It was apparent that she was a hooker. As she got closer, she realized it was the woman who abandoned her baby at Goodwill last week. "Hi. I'm Gloria."

Looking up and down the street, but not at Gloria, she said, "Good for you."

"What's your name?" asked Gloria.

"You a cop?"

"No, I'm not. I just recognize you from Goodwill."

"So?"

"I guess you don't remember me."

"Nope."

"Your baby? You left your baby there. You left her with me."

She stopped looking up and down the street, and looked squarely at Gloria. "I had to. I'm sorry. Is she okay?"

Gloria suggested they have a drink at the bar down the block. She accepted. They talked for nearly an hour. Gloria was shocked by her story of sexual abuse by her father when she was a teenager. She was saddened when she heard of the misery she went through when she was homeless. She wanted to give her money for rehab when she was told about her drug addiction.

"So, you see, I can't take care of a baby. I should have had an abortion, but I couldn't pay for it. I was going to bring her to CPS, but I didn't want to answer all the questions they would have to ask. I was going to drop her on the steps of church. I saw that in a movie once. It was cold and I thought doing that was cruel."

"So Goodwill was your answer?"

"Yeah. That's what they do, don't they? Take care of people, even if they're babies?" She then got up from the table and said, "If I don't get back to work, there will be no food on my table tomorrow." Unceremoniously, she left.

Gloria made several calls the next morning. The Goodwill manager had no idea where they took the baby. The police department told her that she had to go to the precinct to file a request for the information. The person who answered the phone at CPS said she could not divulge any information about the children in their custody. *This is ridiculous,* she thought.

She drove to the CPS offices and was again frustrated by the *can't divulge information* receptionist. "It's really simple. All I want to know is if you have a baby here that was picked-up at Goodwill about a week ago."

"Ma'am, I don't know how to say this any differently..."

"So don't say it. Please find it in your heart to say that you know about the baby." The receptionist looked down, twiddled her pen, and pretended that she needed to do paperwork. Gloria left. She decided her next move was to contact an attorney, or maybe the major. Frustration transformed into anger. Near where she parked her car, she saw two women leaving CPS, each wheeling a stroller. She approached them and asked, "Are these babies in CPS?"

"Yes. We're just taking them for a little walk so they can get some fresh air."

"May I see them?"

"Don't see why not, but please, no touching."

Gloria looked at the first baby. "Could be. I don't know. All babies kind of look alike, don't they?"

"Kind of, I guess."

She looked at the second baby, and at first had the same reaction. She screamed out, "That's her! That's her!"

"That's who?"

"That's the baby that was abandoned at Goodwill." Tears of joy filled her eyes. She ran back to the receptionist and asked what the adoption procedure was."

"Do you have any particular child in mind? Age, sex, race?"

"Definitely. A baby. The one wearing the booties with the hummingbird."

H
e lowered his eye glasses to the tip of his nose and said, "Okay, Seth, let's be original this time. How's the name Jonathan Doe?"

"I like it, Doc. It makes him sound distinguished."

Laughing and coughing, he said, "You mean *extinguished*, don't you?" He brushed off the ash that fell off his cigarette onto his scrubs.

Detective Hammond, an 18-year veteran of the police force, went into the examination room. He was not a fan of Dr. Henry Gilford, but he treated him respectfully. He didn't deserve respect, but he knew Gilford was always uncooperative with anyone that didn't suck up to him. "You're right on time, Detective."

"You mean you've already determined the COD for M-810?"

Speaking as if he cared about dead people, he said, "First, you must pay more respect to those who lay on my tables. He is not M-810. He is Mr. Jonathan Doe."

"Okay, sure."

Gilford took a puff of his cigarette and then cut off the lit tip with surgical scissors. The smoldering tobacco fell to the cadaver's leg. Seth brushed it off. Gilford placed the unlit portion of the cigarette in his pocket. "Waste not, want not."

"You said, 'first.' Is there a second?"

"COD is a nine-millimeter. Brain. Hole in front, out the back." He threw up his hands and said, "Whallah!"

Hammond slowly shook his head back and forth, cleared his throat and asked, "Did you find anything else that might be useful in my investigation?"

"Yes, he hasn't taken a bath for at least a month, maybe two. Does that help?"

"No other trauma? No bruises? No cuts? No needle marks?"

Gilford leaned across the table towards Hammond. "Do I detect, Detective, a note of disrespect? Are you suggesting I don't know how to do my job?"

Not seen by Gilford, Hammond made a fist. He wanted to punch the overweight, slovenly dressed coroner, but contained his anger within his hand. "No, Doc. Didn't mean to offend. Just thought you've been so busy lately that..."

With a pompous air, Gilford said, "You're forgiven. If there's nothing else, have a good day." He pointed his scissors at the exit door.

Hammond's fist remained clenched. *One punch, just one punch and I will have a good day*, he thought, but keeping his job was more important.

At Gilford's direction, Seth wheeled the body into the freezer. Hammond noticed that Seth was wearing flip-flops. He thought that was unusual footwear for the job he had, but then again, he always thought Seth was a weirdo.

"Careful you don't trip, Seth."

Seth looked down, thinking that there was something on the floor. He gave Hammond a questioning look. Hammond responded with a simple snort, and left.

The next evening, Hammond arrived at the scene and took a quick look at the body of a young Black man, dressed as if he was out for a jog. He thought, *Ugly sneakers, but maybe they're good for running.* He turned to the police officer and asked, "Any witnesses? Anything?" The officer told him that he was found about nine-thirty, just after Goodwill closed. He was found by a guy that works there.

"Where is he?"

The officer pointed, and said, "That older guy, over there."

"I'm Detective Hammond. What can you tell me about the dead guy over there?

"Hello, Detective. My name is Christopher. All I can tell you is that when I left Goodwill, I saw a body, that body. "I determined that he was deceased and called 911."

"Have you ever seen him before?"

"Yes. In Goodwill. I remember his sneakers."

"Did you see any other people around him at that time?"

"It didn't look like he was with anyone."

Hammond told Christopher that he might have some more questions at another time, but he could leave if he wanted to. Christopher wanted to, and left.

Several hours later an ambulance arrived and carted the corpse to Gilford's lab.

"Got another one late last night, Roy. Black guy, mid-20s. Looks pretty healthy."

Gilford's much younger cousin, Roy, was in his second year of residency at Bennington Hospital. He was knee deep in debt, and willing to *bend the law,* rationalizing that bending it was not breaking it. "How about that other guy that you've had on ice for a week. That homeless dude?"

Gilford sat in his large, leather desk chair, rocking back and forth. "Let's not go to the dance too soon, young man. I'm still waiting for the cop's sign-off so I can send the body for cremation. Har, har, har."

"You know you're going to get the sign-off. You always do when they can't identify the body."

Gilford lit another cigarette and inhaled deeply. Coughing, he said, "We got a good thing going here. Patience. We have to walk, not run."

Roy was stressed out because of his gambling debts, exacerbated by the insane hours he had to work at the hospital. "Hank. They don't check the freezer to see if the body is still there. You'll get the paperwork. I need the cash."

Gilford stopped rocking. He smashed his newly lit cigarette into the ashtray, leaned forward over the desk, and screamed into the phone. "Look, you little shit." He paused, sat back, and regained his composure. With a calmer voice he said, "I apologize for calling you a little shit. You're just a dumb shit. You gamble, I don't. You lose, I don't. We will continue to do things my way." He then barked, "*Get it?*"

"Sorry, Cous. You're right. Call me when you can."

The call ended. Gilford yelled out, "Seth!"

Seth went into his office. "What's up?" he asked.

"Did you put all of Mr. Jonathan Doe's clothing in one of those nice plastic bags that the city graciously gave to us?"

"Yup. Shoes and all."

"Wrong size?"

"Yup. And ugly. No pizazz to them."

"You're an excellent diener, my friend, but the cheapest guy I know."

———◦((◦))◦———

Three days later, Hammond returned to Gilford's office. "Well, Doc, here's the release for M-810."

"I'm sure Mr. Jonathan Doe will be delighted."

"Couldn't find anything about that guy, and couldn't find anyone who knew him."

Gilford screamed out, "Seth!" Seth came into Gilford's office. Gilford handed him the release form. "You know what to do."

"We're still looking into the guy that came in a couple of days ago. The Black guy."

"Yes. I decided to name him J. Black Doe. It has kind of a nice ring to it, don't you think?"

"Yeah, sure. Whatever you say." He looked at the tag on the corpse's toe, and said, "But I'm a numbers guy, so I'll stick with M-811."

Hammond asked Gilford to speculate on why there were so many John and Jane Does lately. Seth wanted to say, "Because they're cash cows." Gilford answered with, "We live in violent times, Detective. Anything else you need?"

Hammond sucked in his lips, and gave a quick

'no' nod. "Nope. Adios." Walking out, he had the ee-rie feeling that something wasn't right. He couldn't put his finger on it. He stopped at the doorway, turned, and raised his index finger as if he was about to ask one more question. Neither Gilford or Seth said any-thing. An awkward silence ended after a few seconds when Hammond bent his finger with a goodbye mo-tion. Hammond had a strange feeling that he was miss-ing something. *Hmm,* he thought. *Something tells me something's not right. Maybe I just want something to be wrong so I can tell Gilford what I really think about him.*

When Hammond was out the door, Seth texted Roy: "Tonight 8 confirm." Within seconds he received Roy's confirmation. Seth then texted Marvin: "Doe to-night 9. Confirm." A minute later he received a reply from Dignity Funeral Home: "Confirm."

Roy arrived as scheduled, and donned scrubs, gloves, and eyewear he stole from the hospital. He carefully dissected Johnathan Doe, making sure that the cuts were surgically precise. Roy's goal was two-fold: Keep each body part as pristine as possible, and practice his surgical skills.

Seth placed each piece of the cadaver into a trash bag and tagged the contents. The bags were placed in the freezer, awaiting Marvin's arrival.

Having performed dismemberment many times, it took Roy little time to finish his task. "I think I broke my record, Cous." He looked at his watch and said, "28 minutes. New record!"

Gilford guffawed and said, "I'll go get a trophy for you. I'll inscribe it *Cut-up Man of the Year.*" Seth laughed. Roy didn't.

Roy removed all of his surgical attire and put it in the plastic bag that contained the cadaver's belongings. "When's the pick-up, Seth?"

Seth looked at his watch. "In about 20 minutes."

"I can't wait. I have to get back to the hospital. Graveyard shift. Hank, you think I could get paid now so I don't have to come back tomorrow?"

Gilford bowed his head, looked over his eyeglasses with a stern expression, and said, "I don't know how much the trophy is going to cost, so after I buy it, I'll give you your cut. Now get the hell out of here!"

Roy departed. Seth cleaned up. Marvin arrived. The bagged body parts were placed in Marvin's large portable freezer. As Marvin wheeled the freezer to his hearse, he said, "Perfect timing. I got a call this morning from a medical guy...well, maybe he was a medical guy. He wanted these exact parts from this kind of man."

Gilford said, "We're here to serve. And we're here to make some money, so be sure you're paid in cash. Adios."

When Seth finished cleaning, he offered an idea to Gilford. "Why don't we do it all? Cut Marvin out. Sell the Does ourselves?"

"The only way we can get caught is if a buyer reports us. They deal with Marvin. If they're not happy with the product, they piss on Marvin, not on us."

"Gotcha. Smart. Very smart."

<hr>

A few days later Hammond went to Gilford's lab.

"We identified M-811 based on his fingerprints. Wayne Stogsdill. You were probably right that the COD was drugs."

"Probably?"

"I mean our investigation confirmed that he was into drugs. Big time. He was in prison for drug trafficking and just got out last month."

Clearly being sarcastic, Gilford said, "How sad. A life ruined by drugs. Imagine."

He cleared his throat, took a puff of his cigarette, and blew out the smoke, disregarding that Hammond was only a couple of feet away from him. "Have you arranged for his family to identify the body?"

Hammond waved the smoke away from his face and said, "Can't do that. No family. In fact, no one we talked to in his neighborhood knew him. Looks like you have another cremation to take care of."

Gilford screamed out, "*Seth!*"

"Yes, Doc?"

"This nice detective told me that J. Black Doe was known as Wayne Stogsdill when he was alive. I'm sure he enjoyed being our guest, but he's checking out."

Seth started laughing and tried to talk at the same time. "He already checked-out, and now he's check-ing out again." Neither Hammond or Gilford laughed at Seth's lame joke.

Hammond noticed that Seth was wearing a pair of expensive-looking sneakers. Their distinctive multi-col-ored pattern was unmistakable. They were the same ones he saw on Stogsdill when he was found dead on the street. It caused Hammond to raise an eyebrow, both the one on his face and the one inside his mind. He bid Gilford a good night and left his office. Walking out of the lab, Hammond told Seth, "Hey, Seth, nice sneakers."

Seth didn't smile or say anything. He just looked down at his sneakers, then up, then nodded. Hammond found Seth's reaction somewhere between interesting and suspicious. Hammond's cop-instinct kicked in. He thought, *What's up? Is Seth feeling guilty about stealing the sneakers from a dead guy?* He dismissed his thoughts as nonsense. *There's nothing here. An egotistical coroner and an assistant acting strangely. Forget it.* As he drove away, one of his favorite movies popped into his head: "Donnie Brasco." That made him utter Johnny Depp's line, "Forgetaboutit." He said it again and again, louder and louder. He stopped talking to himself, but his mind didn't turn off. He told himself, "I can't forgetaboutit."

Hammond decided to stake out the lab. On the first night he watched the comings and goings of various people. Around seven o'clock the lab lights went out. Seth and Gilford left the building. Hammond went home. On the second night, ditto.

On the third night the lab lights stayed on. At eight o'clock an old Chevy pulled up. A young guy wearing scrubs went into the building. Less than an hour later, he came out and drove away. Moments later a hearse pulled up. A tall, thin, middle-aged guy pulled a large box out of the hearse and wheeled it inside the lab. Five minutes later the guy came out and put the large box back into the hearse. He drove away.

Hammond followed the hearse which eventually pulled into a parking space at the back of the Dignity Funeral Home. The large box was wheeled into the building. Hammond decided it would be best to get a search warrant and return in the morning.

The following morning Hammond and a couple of police officers paid a visit to Marvin, search warrant in hand. Hammond quickly found the large box that Marvin wheeled in the night before. It was empty. He instructed Marvin to unlock what appeared to be a large, built-in freezer.

Inside the freezer Hammond spied a couple of dozen trash bags. He opened one marked "Head." He yelped when he saw Johnathan Doe's eyes looking at him. He decided he didn't need to open up any other bags.

Marvin fully disclosed that he purchased body parts from Gilford, and sold them to medical researchers and the like. The 'like' was never discovered. He was cuffed and Mirandized, despite his statements that it was legal to sell body parts. Hammond did discover that Marvin was right. Selling body parts was legal. *How* the body parts were obtained was another matter. Hammond also thought that the IRS would be interested in Marvin's cash flow.

Hammond's second stop was at the coroner's office. He was greeted by Gilford. "Well, well, well, Detective. To what do I owe this honor?"

"The only honor you'll be facing is when you see a judge and say, "Your Honor, I'm innocent.""

Hammond jerked his handcuffs off his belt and told Gilford he's under arrest for illegally harvesting and trafficking human body parts. He cuffed and Mirandized him; a police officer did the same to Seth.

Gilford knew that Hammond would track-down Roy. He also knew that his spineless cousin would turn state's evidence on him. He needed to warn him. Indignantly, he said, "I'm entitled to a phone call."

"You'll get that at the precinct, you fat, arrogant, smelly, pompous, piece of shit!"

"I seem to be a man of many adjectives, Detective."

"You're also a man who'll be described with a noun: convict."

Roy was arrested at Bennington. All of the staff that saw Roy handcuffed and escorted out of the hospital assumed he was arrested for stealing drugs. They thought Roy was a nice guy and a good doctor. They all wished him well in court, but changed their minds when they discovered why he was arrested.

—————«◉»—————

A few days later Christopher read the morning newspaper while he drank black coffee in Goodwill's donation area. He uttered a *hmm* once or twice as he read the story under the headline: "Coroner Arrested for Body Snatching." All of the reporter's questions were answered by Hammond, to the extent that he was allowed to answer them.

Christopher found one of Hammond's answers to be the most interesting…the most telling. The reporter wrote:

"When asked what happened that gave him the idea that a crime was being committed, Detective Hammond said it was a pair of sneakers."

Christopher read that sentence a second time, smiled, and said, "I know. I know."

My Little Girl

A my shook her head vigorously, clearly signaling that she didn't want to wear the dress her mom picked out. Her mom took another dress from the closet and held it up. Another vigorous *no* nod. Then another. "Well, my sweetie, you decide what you want to wear to church today." Amy chose blue jeans and a T-shirt that was imprinted with "Amy Rules!"

"It's church, sweetie. We have to wear something really nice." Amy pointed to the jeans and shirt, and grunted. Her face seemed to plead with her mom to let her wear what she wanted to wear. "You win. You always win, don't you?" Her mom gave Amy a hug and told her to go get ready.

On the way to church Amy sat in the back seat looking out the window. Every now and then she would turn her head and body around to keep looking at something in particular that the car had just passed. "What did you see?" asked her mom. Amy just pointed backwards, without saying a word.

Her dad pulled into the parking lot, parked, and the three of them walked up the steps to the church. They sat in a pew near the back of the church in case they needed to make a quick exit. Amy sat quietly. The priest spoke, the organ played, and the congregation sang. During the singing her mom thought she heard

Amy mumbling, as if Amy was trying to sing along. Amy wasn't. Amy was merely uttering unintelligible sounds. Now 7-years-old, Amy had never spoken. The last hymn was sung, the priest blessed the congregation, and all departed.

"That was an inspiring sermon that Father Baylor gave," said Amy's mom. Amy's dad kept his eyes on the road and simply nodded in agreement. "Did you like it, Amy?" Amy didn't answer, and kept looking out the window. "Did you like the singing?" Amy didn't respond. Her mom started humming "Here I Am, Lord." She loved the message in the hymn, and indeed did surrender to God. Her faith gave her the courage and commitment to love and care for Amy, despite having a non-verbal child with autism. "Charlie, listen! Stop the car! Listen!"

Charlie stopped. "Listen to what, Meg?"

"Amy. She's singing."

Charlie listened, but didn't hear Amy singing. All he heard was Amy's speech-like utterances. "Meg, I know you would like to think that she's starting to talk, but you know the chances of that are slim to none."

"I'll take slim, Charlie."

———— ((◦)) ————

Amy wore the same jeans and T-shirt the next day. At bedtime she put them on the foot of her bed. Her mom sang a verse from "Swing Low, Sweet Chariot." Amy was snuggled tightly under her blanket. Only her very pretty face was visible. Her eyes were riveted on her mother as her mom sang *A band of angels coming after me, coming for to carry me home."* Her mom bent over to kiss her goodnight. Amy pulled her hand out from under the covers and patted her mother's lips. "More? You want me to sing more?"

Amy nodded, and Meg kept singing. She wanted to call out to Charlie to come to the bedroom. She wanted Charlie to hear what she was hearing: Amy was humming, almost in tune with her. After a couple of minutes of singing, Amy's eyes closed and she fell asleep. Meg picked up the jeans and T-shirt to put in the laundry room.

When morning came, Amy came downstairs for breakfast, wearing the same jeans and T-shirt she wore the last two days. Part of loving Amy was giving in to Amy if the giving was helpful and not harmful. "You win again, sweetie." They ate breakfast the way Amy liked to eat. Each item was placed on a different plate. One type of food never touched another type of food. She ate everything placed in front of her, in order – a bite of toast, a forkful of eggs, one piece of fruit, and a swallow of milk. Meg said to Amy, "Let's go shopping today after school. I just thought it would be really nice to buy you a couple of pairs of new jeans and some T-shirts." Amy jerked her head forward, telling her mom that she agreed. "Go brush your teeth, and put on your shoes."

"Charlie, I had the weirdest dream last night." She told Charlie that she was tending the flowers in her garden and heard a thudding sound from the house. She looked up and saw Amy at her bedroom window pounding on the glass. It seemed Amy was yelling "I'm here. I'm talking to you. Can't you hear me?"

Charlie said, "I'm not Sigmund Freud, but my guess is that you envisioned that Amy knows she can't talk, but wants to talk. She's screaming out for help."

Meg agreed that Charlie was not Freud. "Maybe you're right, Charlie. Maybe not. Either way I still love you." Charlie said he had some errands to run and would be back right after lunchtime.

Amy came downstairs – jeans and T-shirt, sans shoes. "Amy, you need to wear shoes. Please go get a pair." Amy's vigorous 'no' nod told Meg that she had a dilemma on her hands. If she allowed Amy to go shoeless, she might injure herself, to say nothing about the school not allowing her in. If she insisted that Amy wear shoes, there was the strong probability that Amy would scream, thrash around, and perhaps break something. She poured another cup of coffee for herself, sat at the kitchen table, and thought it through.

Grabbing several ribbons from her sewing supplies, she marched upstairs with Amy in hand. She took a pair of sandals out of Amy's closet, and asked Amy which of the ribbons she liked best. Amy chose the red ones. Meg got to work tying the ribbon onto the sandals. She invited Amy to help, and she was enthusiastic about helping. The ribboning was done. Amy slipped into the sandals and energetically nodded 'yes.'

Off to school they went.

A few blocks from the school Amy became very agitated. Meg saw her in her rearview mirror pointing straight ahead and up a little. "What's there, Amy? What is bothering you?" It then dawned on Meg that Amy was pointing to the sneakers hanging from the electrical line that crossed the street. Amy turned around in her seat as they passed under the sneakers, continuing to point and utter sounds. "That looks funny, doesn't it? Why in the world would somebody tie sneakers together and throw them up there?" Not surprisingly, Amy didn't answer, so Meg answered for her. "It's one of those curious things that we will never understand."

━━━➤◄(◍)►◄━━━

A new store opened in the mall. Meg thought it was the perfect place to shop for Amy. "Amy, do you want to look around in "My Little Girl"? Amy gave a slight nod, grabbed her mother's hand and tugged on her as they entered the store. Meg went over to the dresses, but didn't have a chance to look at them. She succumbed to Amy's hand pulling her away. She went to the blouses and tops section. Another pull. "Where do you want to go?"

Amy brought her to the pants rack. She let go of her mom's hand, and slid the hangers down the line, one after another. She stopped at a pair of jeans that looked just like the jeans she was wearing, but they were red, not blue. She pulled them off the hanger and handed them to her mother. Further down the rack, yellow jeans were pulled off and handed to her mother. "Two's enough for now, Amy. Let's see what they have in T-shirts."

Amy did her sliding of hangers and found two T-shirts, one with a simple *Smiley Face* on it, and the other with *"Amazing Grace"* written on it. Meg knew Amy could not read. She guessed that Amy chose the second T-shirt because bright gold writing was on top of a bed of beautiful flowers, and she thought it just looked pretty.

Meg decided shopping in that store was finished, until Amy yanked her over to the shoes. Meg was confused why they were there. *Has Amy changed her mind about wearing shoes?* A kind-faced elderly gentleman was looking through the shoes. When Meg approached, he said, "Perhaps you can help me. My name is Christopher. I want to give a child a present. I know she needs shoes so I thought of buying her a pair. I think she's a size 12, and I know she likes colorful things."

Amy reached-up to touch his shiny, wavy white hair. She stroked it gently, as if she was caressing it. Meg gently said, "Amy, don't do that."

"It's fine, ma'am. I think a lot of kids find my hair rather beautiful if I do say so myself." He laughed, and so did Meg.

Meg said she would be happy to help him. She picked up a pair and handed them to Christopher. He looked at Amy's expressionless face. "Hmm, they're nice, but maybe I should look at another pair." Meg handed him another pair off the shelf. Again, he looked at Amy. Her eyes seemed more open. Her lips slightly parted. "Yes, I think these will be perfect. I think I'll look around for other things too before I make up my mind. Thank you."

Amy pointed eagerly at the same colorful shoes that Christopher chose. She grunted and kept pointing. Meg had her try them on and knew she had to buy them. Amy was jumping up and down with joy. She looked at the name of the manufacturer. She never heard of them, but thought their name was interesting. It read "thomasshoes." The letter "t" was lower case and bolder than the other letters. It struck Meg that the "t" looked like a Christian cross.

Amy pranced and danced around the family room when her father got home. He gave her a hug and a kiss, and said, "I like your red pants, and your T-shirt. And those are the most beautiful shoes I ever saw." Amy jumped up and down a little, and then continued prancing and dancing. It was clear that she was a very happy little girl.

"I'm pretty sure she spoke again, Charlie. Well, not speech-spoke, but she attempted to speak."

"Meg, it breaks my heart too, but we have to be realistic. Amy might never speak. The flash cards have been working for her, and that new digital talking typewriter thing we're going to buy just might be the answer."

Meg patted Charlie on the cheek, smiled, and said, "I am realistic, and I'm also hopeful. The therapist said there's a 50% chance that Amy might be able to talk as she gets older."

Charlie responded, "Honey, optimism is wonderful, but you need to look at the other side. 50% of non-verbal children will just never speak." Charlie hugged Meg, and said, "Let's keep trying. Let's keep looking for solutions. But let's also know that a solution might not be found."

Dinner was eaten and dishes were washed. Amy chipped in with the washing, but never liked to dry them. When finished, she went to her desk in the family room to play video games on the computer. Meg and Charlie watched TV. The evening was a typical, pleasant evening. Bedtime came for Amy. This time Charlie decided to do the talking-hugging-kissing-sweet dreams ritual. As Amy was getting into bed, he noticed she had her pajamas on, and also her new shoes. He lovingly said,

"Amy, how about we put your new shoes under the bed so they can also go to sleep?" Amy quickly bent her knees and pulled her feet back so the heels were resting against her butt. "Hmm," said Charlie. "I guess they'll just have to sleep with you. Good night, baby."

———◦《◉》◦———

Meg called up to Amy, "Breakfast, sweetie. Come on down."

Charlie said, "You sound like that guy on the game show, who was it? Bob Barker? who used to say *Come on down!*"

"Yeah, Bob Barker. Loved that guy. I always wished I could be on that show and win a prize."

"And what prize would you want to win? A vacation? A refrigerator? A new car?"

Meg paused. She had only one prize in mind, and it wasn't anything materialistic. Just then Amy came into the kitchen. "Good morning, sweetie," said Meg.

"Good morning, baby," said Charlie.

In a slow and very deliberate way, Amy said, "Maaa. Daaa."

MONDAY

Wanda greeted Robin when she arrived at the office. "Nice dress, Robin. Is it new?"

"Why yes, it is. Thank you. Wanda."

In the breakroom, Annabella also greeted Robin. "Can I pour some coffee for you?"

"Yes. Thank you."

"I like your dress. Get it at Macy's?"

"Good guess. Yes."

Charlotte walked into the breakroom. "Hey gals, how's the coffee this morning?"

Annabella said, "Hot."

While pouring her coffee into her "I Love You, Mom!" mug, Charlotte asked Robin, "My guess is that you got that dress on sale, right?"

"You're a mind reader, Charlotte. Yes, I did."

Charlotte responded, "No, I'm just literate."

Robin's face gave one of those *Huh?* looks as she walked out of the breakroom, but she wasn't looking where she was going. She bumped into a table and spilled some of her coffee. *"Rrrhh"* she said, as she placed her cup on the table and then wiped the floor with a paper towel.

Robin had many positive attributes. She was an attractive gal in her mid-20s, who had a heart of gold, a first-class mind, and a great sense of humor. On the not so positive side, if anyone searched for the definition of *clumsy*, Robin's photo would be next to it.

Robin's day proceeded pretty much like most of her days at the office. At five o'clock she packed up and took the bus home. She entered her apartment and called out, "Bob, I'm home." Bob just laid on the bed and ignored Robin. Robin called again, "Hey, Bob, are you home?" She didn't get a response. She went to the cupboard and pulled out a can of tuna pâté. When Bob heard the lid snapping off, and smelled the fish, he scampered into the kitchen. If a cat was able to speak, Bob would have said: "Next time don't pull the tab so hard and my pâté won't land on the floor."

She kicked off her heels, unzipped her dress, and took it off. "Ugghh!" she exclaimed when she saw that she forgot to remove the Macy's *Clearance* tag. She put on her Japanese silk robe and went back into the kitchen. She uncorked a bottle of zinfandel and was looking forward to relaxing and decompressing. While pouring the wine into a glass, she stepped on the cork that had landed on the floor. Slightly losing her footing, she also lost some of the wine as it splashed on the counter. After cleaning the spill, she purposely and very carefully walked to her sofa to sit down and enjoy her wine.

TUESDAY

Robin was the only passenger on the elevator and thought she might have been running late. Checking her watch, she realized she was running ahead of schedule. The elevator doors closed, and continued up to the top floor. She saw the lights flashing above the door: 1,2,3,4,5,6,7,8...*Uh oh,* she thought. She forgot to press the 7, so she did, but it was too late. 9 lit and binged. She decided to go to the top floor and pressed 12. When the door opened on 12 a man was waiting to get on, and stepped aside so she could exit. She said, "I'm going down, thank you."

"Okay," he said and got on. She then pressed 7. The doors closed. "Did you forget to press your floor on the way up?"

"No, I just enjoy riding the elevator. It's a pick-me-up in the mornings."

"Patrick."

"Pardon?"

"My name is Patrick."

She looked at him, without responding. The door opened on the seventh floor. She continued to look at him, staring at his blue eyes and brown wavy hair. When he smiled, he had the feeling that she was staring at his teeth. His feeling was right. "Do I have something stuck in my teeth?"

She shook her head and said, "No, no, no. I'm sorry. Your teeth are great. So are your eyes and hair. I mean..." She felt embarrassed by what she was saying and decided getting off the elevator was her only recourse. The door started to close and she dashed out. "Whew! Oh no!" Her handbag got caught in the elevator door. She tugged on the strap. It broke on one side, but then the door opened and she was able to retrieve it. Luckily, the few contents that fell out landed in the corridor, not in the elevator. Kneeling down she picked up what had dropped out, and then saw a pair of men's shoes.

"Good morning, Robin," said her supervisor. "May I ask why you got off a *down* elevator, not an *up* elevator?"

Robin packed her handbag, got up, and said, "Well, you know. What goes up must come down." She quickly walked to her desk, avoiding any other questioning, She placed her handbag on her desk when Charlotte passed by.

"Hey, gal, how are you this morning?"

"Good, Charlotte. I just had the strangest encounter. I saw my ex, Brian, on the elevator as an older guy. Same eyes and hair, and very much the same smile."

"Twilight Zone?"

"No," said Robin pensively. "Just old thoughts."

Charlotte put her hand on Robin's shoulder, and said, "I guess memories of love lost lingers longer than anyone would like."

"Yeah, they do. And that's a lot of 'L' words!"

Charlotte picked-up Robin's hint to change the conversation, and said, "Nice handbag. Big, but nice."

"Nice, but the strap broke."

"No prob, deary. I have some glue that will do the trick until you have it professionally fixed." Charlotte returned moments later and gave Robin a tiny bottle of very strong, almost instant drying glue. "This stuff is extra strong, so be careful."

"Thanks. You're a peach." Robin had a few minutes till the official start time of her job, so she set-out to fix her handbag. She thought, *Wow! Charlotte was right. Extra strong.* Having a little itch on her cheek, she rubbed it with her finger. The itch went away, but her finger didn't. It was stuck to her cheek. She pulled gently, but it remained stuck. She didn't want to yank it off in case her cheek skin came with it. She thought nail polish remover would do the trick, so she scurried back to her desk to get some. She saw her boss coming her way and didn't want to confess that she was careless with the glue.

He noticed that she was typing with only one hand. "You look like Rodin's "Thinker," he said. "Isn't it easier to type with two hands?"

"Yes, it is, but I have a bad toothache and pushing my finger on it helps."

"Sorry to hear that. Can you bring me up-to-date on the past-due accounts?"

"Sure, but if you don't mind, I have to pay a visit to the ladies' room." Back in the ladies' room she rubbed on the remover which dissolved the glue, allowing her to once again have the freedom of all of her fingers. She washed her cheek vigorously with soap, dried her face, and got back to work. "All set," she said.

"That tooth might be inflamed. Your cheek is all red."

"No, no, it's fine. Feeling much better." He asked her to call-up the file on her monitor. When she hit the keyboard, she noticed that a small piece of the paper towel was stuck under her fingernail. She recited what was on the monitor while she kept her hands under her desk, trying to peel off the paper. She succeeded, but also discovered that she ripped off her acrylic nail. She quickly stopped pointing with her nail-missing left hand, and reverted to pointing with her fully-nailed right hand. In making the quick hand switch she knocked over the desk caddy. Paperclips, rubber bands, stickies, pens, and pencils took a journey to the floor.

"Robin, perhaps we can continue this a little bit later. Your tooth is obviously bothering you."

Smiling, feeling awkward, and looking embarrassed, Robin said, "Yup, later. Got it. See ya. Thanks. Back to work."

WEDNESDAY

Robin got on the elevator and was focused on pressing the button for the 7th floor. She was determined to not go up to 12 again. As the elevator filled, Robin stepped to the back. A guy called out, "Hold it please." He got on the crowded elevator and couldn't see or reach the floor buttons. "Could someone please press 7?"

Robin was in the back of the elevator. She was pleased that she was able to say, "It's already pressed."

Bing. The door opened on the 7th floor. She cried out, "Getting off." A few people stepped aside, but only a little bit. "Getting off, please." They huddled closer, but not close enough, so she pushed her way through the press of people and managed to exit. Unfortunately, her heel got stuck on the slight opening between the door and the corridor. She couldn't pull her foot up to release the heel, so she slipped her foot out of the shoe, bent down, and yanked it up. She got the shoe out just in time, and luckily, the heel didn't break. Her boss happened to be at the site. He said, "What goes up must come down, right?"

Robin smiled, rose from the floor, and said, "And what goes down usually comes up."

Wanda passed by just as Robin got up. With a slight giggle she said, "You don't have to bow for your boss, Robin. A simple 'good morning' usually works."

In a friendly manner, Robin said, "Very funny,

Wanda. Oh, and a simple 'good morning' to you." She started to slip her foot in her shoe and lost her balance. Her boss caught her before she fell.

Wanda said, "Okay, a simple good morning is not enough. A hug and a 'good morning boss' are probably best." All three laughed.

The day wore on without any other disturbing or stressful incident. On her way home on the #22 bus, she pondered why she was so clumsy, and what she could possibly do about that. She couldn't muster any solution.

THURSDAY

During a coffee break, she visited the ladies' room. After washing her hands, she took her glasses off, placed them on the shelf above the sink, and gently rubbed her eyes with some water. When she went to put her glasses back on, she fumbled with them and a lens fell out. Back at her desk she used a couple of rubber bands to hold the lens on the frame.

"New shades, Robin?" asked Annabelle.

Robin gave her a slight smile, and said, "They're the latest fashion, sweetie. Everyone in the know is wearing them."

Robin was able to work without further incident during the morning. The rubber bands worked in holding the lens in, but she decided to get her glasses fixed during the lunch break. She went to the Vision-Is-Us down the block. When she was going in, Patrick was coming out. "Brian?"

"No, Patrick."

"Oh, sorry. Yes, Patrick. Hello again."

"I was thinking about getting a pair of those. I kind of like the look, and how helpful they might be if you ever needed a rubber band in a hurry."

Robin laughed at his sense of humor. She held out her hand and said, "Robin."

He shook her hand and said, "See ya."

She smiled and said, "Yeah, and I'll see you better without rubber band marks on your face."

"Gotta go, Robin. A pleasure meeting you, and hope we meet again. Bye."

"Bye."

Back at the office building, the elevator door opened on the seventh floor. Robin was greeted by her fellow staffers with cheers, clapping, and "Happy Birthday!" She was pleasantly surprised and very appreciative. A birthday cake awaited her in the conference room where all gathered. There was a small flashlight sticking up in the middle of the cake, which Robin found interesting. She thought about it for a moment, and said, "Got it, guys. You don't trust me with fire and I agree." Her co-workers...her friends at work...cheered and sang *Happy Birthday*. Her best friend, Charlotte, at work and everywhere else, gave her a long and loving hug.

Robin removed the flashlight from the cake and mimicked blowing it out when she turned it off. Robin picked up the knife to cut the cake into slices, and noticed that people took a step backwards. She laughed and said, "Come on, guys, I can handle a knife. Watch." Deftly, she cut many small pieces of cake, and with Charlotte's help, placed them on paper plates. Her boss came up to her and wished her a happy birthday. She lifted a paper plate, and the edge bent. The cake landed on her boss's shoe. He looked down, then looked up at Robin. In a scolding voice he said, "Robin!" Her eyes opened wide. "Nah, just kidding. My shoes needed a shine anyway."

Robin gave him a kiss on the cheek. He gave her a kiss on the cheek. "Nice having you with us, Robin."

FRIDAY

Deep in thought, Robin was perusing various customer accounts on her computer. She was startled when her cell phone beeped, notifying her of a text message. The message from her sister said, "Sam proposed!!!!!" Robin was ecstatic. She raised her arms and screeched out *yes* as she rolled her desk chair backwards. It bumped into the cubicle's wall, knocking down the shelf on the other side of the wall, along with the books that were on it. Annabelle screamed when she heard the crash. Robin ran to her to make sure she wasn't hurt. She wasn't. "Whew."

"No problema, Robin. Are you okay?"

Robin told her about her sister's news as both of them re-hung the shelf and put the books back. Annabelle said, "Do you have any nails?"

"Nails?"

"Yeah. I thought I'd nail the shelf in case you got any more good news." They ended the incident with laughter and an air kiss.

Robin noticed that the clothes she was wearing for the last month or so seemed tighter. *Gotta get back to exercising,* she thought, and decided to jog on Saturday. On Saturday's she used to take a two-mile jog in a park near her apartment, but hadn't done so for months. *Sneakers. I need a new pair of sneakers* she thought.

Having seen the "Clearance" sign on Dodd's Shoe-a-Rama when she was taking the bus to work, she decided to go there after work.

Having been successful in finding the sneakers she wanted, and at a very low price, she hopped on the bus to go home. Christopher approached her, and said, "May I sit next to you?"

"Be my guest, replied Robin."

Looking at the shopping bag sitting on Robin's lap, he said, "New shoes?

"Actually, sneakers, or more precisely, they're running shoes."

Christopher tilted his head back, took a deep breath, and said, "Ahh, running. I used to run a lot. Now it's called *jogging*. Yeah, I ran and ran, but not always with my head."

"Your head?"

Christopher turned to her. For reasons she couldn't explain, she had the feeling he was a kind and wise man. Perhaps it was his shiny white hair, or cherubic face, or simply his demeanor. She didn't know. "Yes, my head. My feet controlled my mind. I just wanted to do things. Anything. I didn't think things through before I ran through life. When I got older, I realized that I was in control of my feet. I could make them go wherever I wanted them to. I started to think before I ran. Nowadays people say, 'walk before you run.' Same meaning."

"True. I often run before I walk. That's why I'm probably a klutz."

"Klutz?"

Walk in My Shoes - Heartwarming and Inspirational Short Stories

"It seems I'm always dropping things, or tripping, or fumbling. People at work think I'm a walking disaster."

"Hmm," he said. Has that been going on for a long time?"

"No, not too long." She paused and thought about her words. "Make 'not too long' about a year."

"Well, something happened to you a year ago. It's none of my business to know what it was, but it might help if you looked into that."

She pursed her lips and started to think about what happened a year ago. It was the day that Brian called off their wedding and left her.

"My stop is coming up. For what it's worth, keep that thought in mind. You are in charge of where your feet take you. It might be a step at a time, but you'll eventually get where you want to be. Above all, don't run backwards."

"Thank you for your kind words. You're an angel."

Christopher smiled and said, "I get that a lot." Robin watched him as he crossed the street and went into Goodwill.

Saturday

"I'm out of here, Bob." She tied the laces on her new sneakers and out she went to Plaza Park for a two-mile jog. The last time she jogged there was almost a year ago. She fell, badly bruised her knee, and took a hiatus from jogging until it healed. The medical healing happened, but not the mental healing. She was afraid she would fall again, so she had given up jogging.

Now, after a mile on the track that circuited the park

through grasslands, trees, and bushes, Robin started to feel the way she felt before Brian departed.

She completed her run without any accidental fall, rested on the park bench, and hydrated with lots of water. The run was exhilarating and gave her a confidence she hadn't felt for a long time. *That old guy on the bus was right,* she thought. *I just ran forward, not backwards. Forward is how I have to run, how I have to fill my life, how I can be the Robin I used to be.* Any passerby that might have looked at her smiling face would have guessed that she was a very happy person.

One passerby stopped. "Hi there," said Patrick.

Robin looked up, keeping her smile and her feeling of delight, and said, "Hey. Hi. Patrick, right?"

"Yup. You can call me Pat if you'd like. My friends call me Patman, Robin."

A Short Story

___

E arl felt more like a spectator than a player on the basketball court. He was always chosen last to be on the *Skins* or *Shirts* team when the captains of the teams alternated their picks. If there were more than eight kids waiting to be picked, Earl was rarely chosen. It wasn't that they didn't like Earl – they did – and it wasn't that Earl couldn't dribble or pass the ball – he could. At five-feet tall, he was the shortest 13-year-old on the court. He couldn't make a basket from twenty-feet out because he didn't have enough force to shoot from that far away. He couldn't make a basket from right under the hoop because the defense simply held up their hands.

There were only ten teenagers on the asphalt court on that very hot Saturday in Los Angeles. By default, Earl became a player for the *Skins*. He played well, never fumbling the ball, and did an admirable job on defense. The *Shirts* scored a point, and the game was tied at 20-20. Only one basket was needed for the *Skins* to clinch a victory. Peter tossed the ball to Earl. Earl slowly dribbled down the court, surveying who was where and deciding where to run. At the top of the key, he heard Bobby shout out, "Me! Me!" He saw Bobby, hands stretched out waiting for Earl to pass the ball to him. Early also saw an opening right down the middle of the key. He wanted to dribble around the kid that was guarding him so he could get a few feet from the basket and sink it.

Bobby shouted again. "Earl!" Thinking fast, Earl decided to play for the team rather than for his own sense of glory. He passed the ball. Bobby received it, took a jump shot, and it was *nothing but net*. The *Skins* won. None of them minded the sweat on everyone's body as they patted each other and chest-bumped to celebrate their victory. Earl didn't score any points in the game, at least none that appeared on the scoreboard. But he did score points from the four other shirtless kids that appreciated his team spirit.

There were only a dozen spectators at that game. Most of them were the players' classmates; some of them were moms or dads who wanted to see their son play; one was Christopher.

———————————

Earl tapped his father on the head as he rushed out of his home. "I'll be back in a few hours, Dad" His father knew he would be back when he said he would. Earl's mother taught him about kindness, charity, and respect. His father taught him about hard work, responsibility, and commitment. All of the teachings were ingrained in Earl. "Play well, kiddo. Have fun," said his dad.

The Saturday basketball game ended. Earl was again fortunate in getting a chance to play. His team lost, but no one was down because of the loss. All the kids had a great time, as all kids should when playing sports. They even congratulated Earl for scoring one of the baskets.

The high winds that hit their humble home on the outskirts of L.A. caused damage to many homes in the area. A tree fell on one; A *STOP* sign came loose from its pole and smashed through someone's window; a garbage pail was blown into a neighbor's car. Earl's home suffered only slight damage, and a loss. Several roof shingles were turned up and needed to be nailed down. Their small aluminum patio set in the backyard was hurled against their cinder block fence and fell apart. When Earl returned home, he helped his father with the roof, holding the extension ladder firmly on the ground so it didn't wobble. Once completed they drove to In-N-Out for a burger, followed by a visit to Goodwill. While driving there his dad spoke to Earl, recalling several stories of how he and his mother used to sit at that patio table and talk about this or about that, and just enjoyed being together. He almost teared-up while he was telling Earl some stories. Earl listened attentively, and felt the emotion his dad was feeling.

He wrapped his arms around his dad and pressed his head against his chest. "I miss her too."

They arrived at Goodwill and went into the store.

"Our lucky day, Earl. What do you think of this?" Earl looked at the patio set on display. It was in good shape except for some chipped paint and cracks in all four vinyl seats. "Looks good, Dad. We can wrap the seats with some new stuff, and the paint ain't a problem."

"Like they say on that TV program, The price ain't bad."

"The price is right, Dad."

"Yeah, that's what I said." Earl smiled.

They got a large cart, stacked the table and chairs on it, and wheeled it to the cashier. While pushing the cart, Earl passed the men's shoes on display. He saw a pair of barely-worn high top sneakers. His sneakers were three games away from falling apart. He didn't say anything to his dad because he knew money was very tight, and his need for sneakers had to take a backseat to all of the bills his dad had to pay. Earl wanted to help out at home by getting a job after school, but his dad wouldn't let him. He remembered what his father told him more than once. "You already have three jobs. Making and keeping friends is number one. Number two is education. Last, but not least, is helping me with the chores at home." When his father told him that the first time, Early asked him about his car, and his father told him, "Oh, yeah, four jobs. I like a clean car that is shiny." When Earl and his dad finished shopping, Christopher saw them leaving with the patio set. He also saw Earl eyeing the sneakers.

———— ◈ ————

The following Saturday Earl arrived at the basketball court, fully charged and eager to play another game. Twelve kids showed up. Ten of them were chosen to play. Earl was not among them. He decided to stay and watch the game. He certainly didn't want any of the kids to get hurt and drop out, but he thought if one of them got really tired, he just might have a chance to play. He sat on the grass next to the court, cheering when a great play was made, and uttering *ouch,* when any of the players goofed. He enjoyed watching, and he enjoyed chit-chatting with a couple of his female classmates. Earl saw an old guy sitting on a folding patio chair, watching the game. When he glanced at the man, Christopher waved to him. Earl returned the wave. "Who's that?" asked one of the girls.

"I don't know. Maybe he's somebody's grandfather."

When the game ended Christopher approached Earl. "Hi. You didn't play today."

"Nah, I wasn't picked."

"I saw you play last week. I thought you were pretty good."

"I guess, but the guys want shooters, not handlers."

"Handlers? What's that?"

"They're what you call play-makers. Ya know, the guys that are passing the ball around, looking for the best play. They're fast and hard to defend."

"That's what I saw you doing last week."

"Yeah, that's what I did. That's what I always do. But I'm not that fast. I'm just kinda, well, kinda okay at it. Maybe if I was taller."

Christopher cleared his throat, and said, "Let's start with taller. There was a professional basketball player who played on a couple of NBA teams. His name was Muggsy Bogues. He was 5'3" tall. How tall are you?"

"Five-three."

"Enough said on that subject. Now on to what else you said. Why are you only okay at it?"

The question gave Earl pause. He didn't know how to answer. He thought about what he's done on the court, and couldn't find fault with his play. He also couldn't find anything in his play that stood out.

Christopher understood why Earl couldn't answer. He said, "There are two sayings that come to mind. One about how valuable you are on a team, and the other about what you might need to do."

"I'm listening."

Christopher said, "Albert Einstein, that genius guy, said, 'Strive not to be a success, but rather to be of value.'"

"How can you be valuable if you're not successful?"

"Good question. Last week you weren't a success at shooting. You wanted to be successful, but you didn't sink any baskets. You decided to pass the ball to Bobby who scored the winning point. You proved to be a value to your team."

Earl smiled. He liked what he heard.

"The other quote is from Benjamin Franklin. You know, the guy with the kite and the key? He said 'Practice makes perfect.' So, think about that."

"Yeah, I will. I mean, yeah, you're right. Gotta practice."

"And I also have to go. I have a job that I have to get to."

"Okay. Thanks. Bye."

Earl watched Christopher grab his folding patio chair and walk away. He then turned back. Over his shoulder, Christopher said, "Oh, one more thing I'd like to say to you. You might be five-feet-three on the outside, but I suspect you're seven-feet tall on the inside.'"

———◄(◍)►———

Earl took Christopher's advice to heart, and to action. He practiced dribbling every chance he got. He dribbled a basketball inside the house as he went from one room to another. He dribbled outside the house while he was cleaning up or taking the garbage can to the street. He built footwork rings with rope and exercised on them for minutes on end to increase his acceleration, speed, and balance. He passed his basketball to the fictitious player on the outside wall of his house, over and over again, faster, harder.

A few Saturday games were played. Earl played in two of them, but had to drop out on the third Saturday. He almost fell when part of his sneaker ripped off his sole. As he left, he said, "Sorry, guys. Can't play with busted sneakers."

Earl got on his bike. He wasn't due home for another couple of hours, so he thought he'd go to Goodwill to see if those sneakers were still there and how much they cost. At Goodwill he saw the man from the park. "You again. You're not following me, are you?"

"Gosh, no. I work here. Why are you here?"

"Just want to look at the sneakers I saw here a few weeks ago. Are they still here?"

"Don't know. Let's go look."

Earl spotted the sneakers, and said, "Whew. Still here. Ain't no price on them."

"There *isn't* a price on them."

"That's what I said."

Christopher took the sneakers from him, and said, "Let me take a look. Maybe we forgot to price them."

"Well, if they're more than five dollars I can't buy them."

Christopher smiled, and said, "Today's your lucky day, son. Five dollars. And there's no sales tax at Goodwill."

Earl kicked off his old, partially ripped sneakers, and put on the Goodwill ones. "Amazin' that they're my size. Five dollars?"

"Yup."
"Sold!"

———⚫———

As the Saturdays progressed, with summer on the horizon and the end of the school year approaching, Earl continued to practice. He wanted to be perfect, as Franklin said. He became adept at dribbling where it was nearly impossible to steal the ball from him as he moved around the court. He became highly proficient at passing the ball to open players, doing so very often without a defense player correctly predicting to whom he would make that pass. His shooting skills also improved. He was able to take shots from fifteen, twenty, and sometimes twenty-five feet from the basket and score. He was no longer the last pick or benched when a Saturday game took place.

The last game of the season was upon them. Earl, as usual, tapped his dad on the head as he headed out to the court. "Love you, Dad. See ya later."

"No," said his dad. I've seen you bouncing and throwing that basketball all around the house for the last couple of months. It's about time I saw what you can do on the basketball court."

"You're coming to the game? Great!"

They drove to court in his dad's clean and shiny car. His dad parked, pulled out a folding patio chair that he kept in the trunk, and took a seat on the grass. Christopher arrived a few minutes later and chose a spot next to Earl's dad. "Great kids, aren't they?" said Earl's dad.

"Yes, they sure are. It seems all of them were raised by caring parents. Which one of the kids is yours?"

"The shortest one out there. His name's Earl. He's the one picking the kids he wants on his team."

Arnold sat on the park bench next to the playground, watching the kids play and the mothers talking. He noticed that the mothers would sometimes glance at him while they were chatting. He paid no mind to their looks, until he was approached by a police officer.

"How you doing today, sir?"

Arnold closed his laptop and replied, "Just fine."

"May I ask what you are doing?"

Arnold was never intimidated by authority figures, not his teachers in high school, not by his father, and not by policemen. "May I ask why you are asking?"

The police officer took a casual step backwards. His training suggested that if a person seemed arrogant, or nervous, or objected to a simple non-accusatory question, the person just might pose a threat. "It's not every day that we see a man sitting at a playground looking at the kids playing."

Arnold smiled as he stood up. The officer took another step backward and held his hand close to his baton, but gave no indication that he was about to strike Arnold. "My guess is that those ladies over there thought I was a pedophile and called the cops for you guys to check me out. Right?"

"I'm Officer Gerard. Gerry Gerard. May I ask your name?"

"Arnold. Arnold Timbolt."

In a very friendly manner, Gerard said to Arnold, "Well, you're a good guesser, Arnold. So here I am checking you out. I hope you understand why I have to."

Arnold put his laptop into his soft leather briefcase, and reached for a stack of papers that were bound with a large bulldog paperclip. "We're on the same page, Officer. Let me show you this and I'll explain why I'm here."

When Gerard saw Arnold reaching into his brief-case, he un-cinched his baton, ready to be removed from his duty belt. "Arnold, I'd appreciate it if you just put that briefcase down on the bench."

"You're good, Officer. If I were in your shoes, I'd also be apprehensive." Arnold placed the briefcase on the bench. "I'm just going to slowly reach for a stack of papers. Okay?"

"Okay."

Arnold pulled out his stack and held it up so Gerard could clearly see the top page. It read, "Abandoned."

"So, what are you telling me?"

"I decided to write a novel about kids who are aban-doned by their parents. I'm watching these kids and their mothers in an attempt to get inspiration for how I see things happening. You know, what I should write in my book."

Gerard fanned the pages of Arnold's uncompleted manuscript, and decided to believe him. He never-theless took Arnold's ID, saying, "This is just routine, Arnold. I wish you the very best of luck with your book. I'll go tell the mothers that everything is okay. Would you like to join me?"

Having always felt uncomfortable talking with women, Arnold didn't want to have an encounter with the mothers. As a child, he was shunned by his mother, and chastised if he interfered with her business while she worked in the world's oldest profession. He never felt comfortable with girls, and never had a girlfriend. Now 25-years-old, the uneasiness and awkwardness he felt in the company of women remained. He told Gerard that he had an appointment that he needed to get to. He shook Gerard's hand, thanked him for being a good cop, and left the park.

Arnold was not inspired by his late afternoon visits to the playground. He abandoned "Abandoned," deciding that he needed to write about something else.

The confluence of three circumstances, years apart from each other, put him on his journey to write a novel. He felt abandoned as child; his high school English teacher told him that he was a very good writer and should think about writing a poem; he was fascinated by the concept of introspection which he learned in Psych 1 in college. He believed that if he put his thoughts on paper and then read those words, it would help him better deal with life. At first it was an action plan, but as the months and years passed, it was slowly becoming an obsession.

He walked around the park, looking at people, at squirrels, at pigeons being fed on the path by lonely looking people who tossed crumbs on the ground. He went to the pier down by the river, and watched fishermen casting their rods with the hope of snagging dinner. He watched people boarding their small motorboats and become excited when their boat roared and created a wake. Nothing he saw inspired him.

Saturday came and Arnold decided to walk around a different part of town, the part that he never walked through. He was hopeful that inspiration would strike. He came up dry. A gurgle in his stomach advised him that he was hungry. Twenty minutes after leaving that part of town, he saw *Pancake Palace* and walked in. At three o'clock in the afternoon it wasn't surprising that very few people were there. "Table, booth, or counter?" asked a young lady at the reception area.

"Booth." She escorted him to a booth and placed a menu in front of him. A waitress arrived, pen and pad in hand, and said, "Hi, what can I get you today?"

Arnold looked up from the menu at what he thought was the prettiest woman he ever saw – ever saw close-up. Her red hair beautifully framed her peach-colored complexion. Her green eyes captivated him. He was smitten by her. "Ah…." and he froze. His mouth was agape.

"Need some more time? I'll get you some water." Although he held the menu as if he was reading it, he didn't read it. He saw only her. A minute later she returned to his table. "Ready?"

"Sissy," he said.

"Yes, my name's Sissy. I was lucky this morning and put the right name tag on. Whew!"

Arnold smiled. He thought to say *If your sense of humor was a choice on this menu, I'd pick it,* but he didn't. He wanted to say *I think you are a very beautiful woman*, but he didn't say that either. "Ah, small stack. Blueberry."

"Coffee? Tea? Coke?

"Just water."

Sissy thought Arnold was a good-looking guy, nicely dressed, and, her favorite: clean-shaven. She didn't know why, but she had a warm feeling about him. As she walked away, Arnold pulled out his laptop and was anxious to start typing. He had an idea about a novel. He typed *Title – Meeting a Waitress,* and then typed cryptic notes about what he saw – *Pretty waitress, Sissy, not many customers, red vinyl booths,* and so on.

Christopher was sitting at the table next to the booth. He scooted his chair around to face Arnold, and said, "Writer?"

Arnold looked up. He thought of saying *Why are you asking?* but didn't. He felt something about Christopher that he couldn't decipher, and decided to say, "Yes. Well, trying to be one."

"Do you remember that *Star Wars* movie when Yoda said, *Do or do not. There is no try?*"

"Yeah, I do. You do his accent very well. Funny little guy, wasn't he?"

"Funny, and brilliant." Christopher got up from his chair and asked, "May I join you?" Before Arnold answered Christopher sat down in the booth. Jovially, he said, "I would like to know what you are writing about, unless, of course, it's a plan to rob a bank, or a confidential report about your last CIA spy mission."

Arnold was flattered that someone had an interest in his writings. He closed his laptop, not to hide what he typed, but to pay attention to what Christopher was saying.

"Here you are, handsome. Blueberry small stack. Syrups are on the table," said Sissy.

Arnold blushed and looked embarrassed. He wanted to say *Just trying to get a big tip, right?* but said, "Thank you for the nice words." When she smiled, he thought she lit the room. He felt it down to his core.

For a second or two, which felt like several minutes for both Arnold and Sissy, she stood there, speechless. Her green eyes looked at his blue eyes, and vice versa. Coming out of her daze, she cleared her throat and turned to Christopher. "Would you like me to refill that drink, sir?"

"No need. I must be going. Goodwill awaits me." Sissy went back to the counter. "I'm Christopher, by the way."

Arnold smiled, more out of courtesy than to express joy, and said, "Arnold."

"So, Arnold. I'd like to continue our little conversation tomorrow, if you don't mind. I'd love to know what you're writing about." He saw that Arnold was not paying attention to him. Arnold just kept looking at Sissy. "Arnold? Hello. Anyone home?"

Still looking at Sissy from afar, Arnold inadvertently poured the entire contents of maple syrup on his stack. Christopher knew why he did, and didn't say a word about it. But he did say, "Can we meet tomorrow morning at the Goodwill around the corner? Say ten o'clock? I have something I want to show you."

Arnold, not looking at Christopher, said, "Sure."

———»«(O)»«———

Arnold awakened from a deep sleep. Yawning and stretching, he said to himself, "Wow. Great dream."

His dream involved Sissy. He knew he had to see her again, but his first order of business for the day was to keep his commitment and meet with Christopher. He arrived two minutes before Goodwill opened. A second after his arrival, the door opened, and Christopher said, "Welcome to my domain, Arnold."

"You work here?"

Christopher signaled Arnold to walk with him. "I don't call it work. I help people and feel good about it. Sometimes I inspire people, and I feel very, very good about that."

They arrived at the men's shoe rack and Christopher stopped. "You want me to buy a pair of shoes?"

With a laugh, Christopher said, "No, I just want you to look at them. One pair at a time."

Arnold looked at the shoes, from left to right, from the top rack to the bottom rack. "So now what?"

"Did you see anything interesting, anything that you liked, anything that drew you to the shoes?"

"Nope. Just shoes….and sneakers, boots, and a pair of flip-flops."

"Close your eyes, Arnold, and pick one of the shoes. Just one." Arnold did. "Let's go to the back room."

In the donation area Christopher slid a couple of rocking chairs together to face each other. "Have a seat, my friend." They sat in rockers for about a minute, just rocking back and forth. "I'd like you to close your eyes again."

"This is getting to be a little weird, Christopher."

"Yes, I know what you mean, but I'd like you to trust me on this." Arnold closed his eyes. "Do you remember when you told Officer Gerard at the playground that you wanted to see how things happened?"

Arnold opened his eyes and jolted forward, almost falling off his rocker. "How do you know about that?"

"I know Gerry Gerard. Does that answer your question?" Arnold sat back on his rocker, and nodded 'yes.'

Christopher again instructed Arnold to close his eyes. "Run your fingers around the shoe. Touch every part of the shoe?" Arnold did as he was instructed. "What do you feel, Arnold?"

"Leather, laces, a hard heel, a worn-out sole that's scraped on one of its edges."

"Arnold, what do you feel?"

"I just told you."

"What do you feel inside yourself, emotionally, as you're touching the shoe?"

"I feel relaxed. I like the feeling of rocking."

"Good. What else do you feel?"

"I'm wondering why the shoe is scraped on the side."

"Play it out. Make up a story about it."

"Okay. I see an old man who walked with a limp, dragging his foot as he walked, scraping the sole on the pavement. He's on a lonely street. He feels alone in the world, still grieving over the loss of his wife many years ago. He wants to end his life, but then recalls a memory of his grandchild. He starts to cry."

Christopher saw Arnold's eyes bouncing around under his lids as he envisioned, and felt, a story. "Excellent. Open your eyes, my friend."

"Are you a psychiatrist, Christopher?"

Almost chuckling, he responded, "No, no, no."

"How strange. I was actually feeling what the old man might have felt."

"And how about those kids at the playground? Did you feel what they might have been feeling? Or did you just see what they were doing?"

Arnold didn't have to answer, but Christopher thought reinforcing the answer would help. "When your eyes are opened and your fingers are on the keyboard, you're using your mind and your eyes to say something, something that will make people see something. But you've not been in touch with your own feelings, so the words you are putting on paper are vacuous. You need to feel what is in your heart. Let it out. Put it into words."

Christopher saw that Arnold was looking out into space and digesting what he heard. "Close your eyes, Arnold. Open your heart."

———— ◆ ————

Arnold left Goodwill and went to the *Pancake Palace*. "Booth, table, or counter?"

Arnold didn't answer. He just kept looking around, but didn't see Sissy. "Does Sissy have a particular area that she serves?"

"Yes. Booth or table?"

"Booth." She escorted him to the booth and placed a menu in front of him. He didn't pick it up. He sat there for over a minute, which felt like an hour, looking around for Sissy.

She arrived. "Oh, hi again. Loved our pancakes, did you?"

"Yes, very much. And I loved the service. By the way, I'm Arnold."

She held out her hand to shake his. When their hands met, both of them were still. Again, both of them looked into each other's eyes. Both of them smiled.

Arnold's new routine for after-work hours and weekends became dining at the *Pancake Palace*, each time meeting with Sissy, each time exchanging small talk.

"Sissy, we're getting to know each other, and I don't know about you, but I feel very nice, kinda very comfortable with you."

"Right back atcha."

"When you get off your shift today, would you like to have dinner with me?"

"If it's not here, I'd love to. Make it tomorrow. I'm not working on Sunday." She jotted her address and phone number on a notepad and handed it to him.

He glanced at the notes, smiled, and said, "I'll pick you up at seven."

———((◉))———

The longest shower he ever took was a couple of hours before he was to pick-up Sissy. The hot water rained on him, relaxing his muscles and his mind. As the water flowed down his face, he was flooded with thoughts. *How much should I share with her? If I tell her about my mother, will it turn her off? If I tell her about being awkward with women, will she think less of me? Open-up? Be me? Be honest? Let her do the talking? Keep the conversation about her, not me?* Struggling with the litany of questions he had, and having few if any answers, he decided to simply play it by ear. He got dressed and left for the dinner he very much looked forward to having with Sissy.

After a typical superficial *getting-to-know-you* conversation at the candle-lit dinner table, Arnold took a deep breath, and said, "Sissy, I need to tell you a couple of things about me. If I don't, it would be like lying to you about who I am."

Sissy was impressed by what he said. She had the very warm feeling that the guy sitting at the table with her was a stand-up, honest, genuine person. She said, "I want to hear everything about you."

Arnold confessed about his upbringing and his awkwardness with women. While he talked, they held their hands together across the table. Her eyes were riveted on his, almost as if she was feeling the emotional pain he had gone through. He was mesmerized by Sissy, feeling the warmth of his emotions taking over his mind and body. He didn't feel an inkling of awkwardness.

"I don't know what to say, Arnold. All I can think of is, so what's next?"

"My novel."

"Yes, how's that coming along?"

"Very well, I think. I'd like your opinion on where I'm going with it, if you don't mind."

He pulled out the first ten pages of his manuscript from his suit jacket and handed it to her. "Well, it's a good start before I even start reading it. I love the title: Close Your Eyes and See."

One Shoe

"There's another one. How odd. I always wondered why? How did it get there? Whose was it?"

"What?"

"The shoe"

"What shoe?"

"The one we just passed."

"We passed a shoe?"

"That's what I said. Actually, it was a boot, not a shoe. Why do you have that strange look on your face?"

"Talk about strange looks, you should see yours!"

"What's wrong with my face?"

"The word *weird* is written on your forehead. No, not literally. Stop looking in the rearview mirror. But looking in the mirror does underscore what I said."

"What?"

"You're weird."

"Why does my wondering why there's always, I mean always, only one shoe on the road make me weird?"

"Who the hell cares about a lost shoe, John? And look at the road, not at me."

"I do, Sheila."

"You're looking at me with that smug expression. I didn't mind it when I was your student, but I do now."

"In my philosophy class?"

"No, teaching me how to push the lever down on the toaster."

"Whew. I think Sheila is upset about something."

"My stomach feels like Carlsbad Caverns."

"Hard as rock or riddled with stalagmites and bats?"

"Ha, ha. Empty. I'm hungry. Please find a restaurant."

"You just alleviated my concern. When you were just rubbing your belly, I thought you might have thought you were pregnant."

"Yeah, hunger. I'm still on the pill, you know. Not that it's made any difference for the last several months."

"A pill a day keeps the baby away."

"Sure, make a joke out of it, rather than having an adult discussion."

"You didn't like my slogan?"

"Loved it, John. Just loved it."

"That's a rather snide way of putting it."

"Stop!"

"I don't see a restaurant."

"If you were looking straight ahead rather than at me, you would have seen the stop sign you just went through."

"Whoopsie doodle."

"You're only 35-years-old and you're already suffering from old age. Maybe even dementia. Whoopsie doodle? Really grown up!"

"Let's get back to my philosophy class. I can still remember you when you walked into my class the first time. I watched you walk from the door to your seat. Glide is a more appropriate word than walk. There was something about you that gave me a thrill."

"That thrill was in your pants, wasn't it?"

"You sound very flip about it. Maybe it was in my pants, but also in other parts of my body. My heart, for example."

"Oh, please. Pants, heart. They're the same thing for you."

"You are still gorgeous. I'll add sexy to that. Slim, trim, big green eyes, long and luxurious red hair, and, do I have to say it?"

"No, you don't have to say it. I know I have freckles."

"Ha, ha, ha. Yes, you do have freckles, but not on your..."

"Cool your spurs, Cowboy. Okay, I'm attractive. So are you. You know you're handsome, and you know lots of guys would love to have your black, curly hair. But if you think size matters, all I have to say..."

"So, say it."

"I'm not going to stroke your ego. In fact, I'm not in the mood to stroke any part of your body."

"Here I am trying to have an intelligent conversation...an adult conversation about how we met, and you're acting like an indignant..."

"Indignant what? Whore? Bitch? Scorned lover?"

"Shelia, let's be civil. Lower your voice. I can hear quite well in the car. None of those statements apply to you. You're not a bitch or a whore!"

"Huh! You forgot scorned, John."

"Sheila, I have not scorned you. I don't know how to say this any differently than what I told you many times. You are the only woman in my life. I have never, absolutely never had a relationship with another woman since I met you."

"Dammit! Why did you slam on the brakes?"

"There!"

"Why are you acting so excited? What's there? What are you pointing at?"

"At that sign. The one that says *restaurant.*"

"There must have been a downpour while we were eating."

"Not the best food in town, was it?"

"It has to be. It's the only restaurant in town."

"If we took the highway instead of the backroads, we probably would have had lunch at a better place."

"But the backroads fill our nostrils with the scent of crops growing, and our ears with cows mooing, and our eyes with green grass and trees."

"Your nose and ears and eyes could have done without that, and we would have saved ten hours driving."

"I don't have to meet with the faculty in Coopersville until Monday. We have plenty of time to get there. Besides, we now have more time to talk."

"About what, John? I've tried talking to you for a long time. You either make a joke to divert the conversation, or you're too busy with this or that, and you tell me that it's just not the time."

"We've been very comfortable for the last year. It was the right decision to live together."

"*Was* is the operative word. We got along just great for the year that we were dating. Living together slowly ate away at our happiness. Well, my happiness. I don't know about yours"

"Things changed this last year. Losing my job was

a turning point. Our income was cut by more than half. We had to give up a lot of things."

"Money is not our problem."

"No, I guess not. But I'd rather be one of the *haves*, not the *have nots*."

"John Collins, Professor of the Elite. I can just see it on your business card."

"You're hammering away at my values, my beliefs, my wants, and my character as if I was a rotten, no good, empty shell of a man."

"You got that right. I used to think that you were a solid guy, put together well on the outside, and caring and loving on the inside."

"Sheila, we've had lots of arguments since we've been together. I used to think most of them were just superficial brain games. You know, each of us having a quiver filled with barbs and witticisms, and we'd shoot them at each other to see who could hit the target better."

"That used to be the case, I guess. I didn't think about *why* we argued, why we fought. All I thought about was that I loved you, and I wanted to give you my unconditional love."

"Unconditional? I think it became conditional. I don't know why. I do know we're arguing now and it's a real argument, a fight, like a fight to the death."

"You're gripping the steering wheel like you were choking it, and your body couldn't be more rigid. Maybe we should talk about something else."

"Another one!"

"That's what I said. Let's change the subject."

"And it's a different one. Not a match to the other one."

"Are you losing it, John? What the hell are you talking about?"

"I just saw another shoe. The first one I saw was definitely a boot, not a shoe. They're different."

"Uh-huh."

"Yeah, fine, Sheila. You just sit there with your eyes closed, reclining back on your seat, looking sad and staying quiet."

"I'm thinking, John. The shoes are a fab metaphor."

"Are they also empty inside?"

"Maybe, but it doesn't matter. Think about it. Two shoes..."

"One shoe and one boot."

"Fine. Even better. Think about it. Two pieces of footwear, near each other, having the same reason for being, the same need, yet they don't go together."

"You've just proven that you deserved that 'A' that I gave to you in class. If I hear you right, you're a shoe and I'm a boot. Right?"

"We should have rented a convertible."

"You mean the air is getting kind of thick in here and you need some fresh air?"

"No. It's just that the sky looks amazing. The blue, the white, billowy clouds, and a rainbow."

"And you call me weird?"

"Diversion, John. You used diversion with me in the past. When I hit you with one of those arrows you mentioned, you hugged me, kissed me, fondled me. We wound up making love and I forgot about the arrow."

"I have to back-up."

"Really, John. Let's not rehash what we've gone through. Let's just get where we're going. Why are you stopping?"

"I'm backing up. I want to get that shoe."

"John, from the bottom of my heart, I am asking you to please...please keep going. I'm tired, irritable, and I just want to get there."

"Unbelievable!"

"Give me a break. Why did my asking you to keep going irritate you so much?"

"It didn't. What's unbelievable is what's ahead."

"What?"

"There. See that guy walking?"

"Yeah. So?"

"See what he's carrying?"

"No."

"A shoe! He's carrying a shoe, Sheila!"

⇒⇒«◐»⇐⇐

"Hi. Need a lift?"

"Thank you. My feet could use a rest."

"This is going to sound crazy, but I think I know what you need?"

"Mind reader, are you?"

"No, just good eyesight."

"What did you see?"

"You're carrying a shoe."

"You do have good eyesight."

"Well, sir. I happen to have seen a shoe that looks just like your shoe."

"You found it?"

"Yup. It's back there, about half-a-mile."

"I won't be surprised if that is my shoe."

"Hop in. Rest your feet. I'll take you to it."

"Where are you headed?"

"Just up the road, ma'am. 'bout a mile or so. How about you? Where are you headed?"

"I know where John is headed, but I'm not sure where I'm going."

"Shelia, you're just confusing this nice man."

"I'm not confused. I've been around a long time, as if you couldn't tell by my white hair."

"I apologize for Sheila. She's just not in a good mood. I'm John, by the way."

"I'm not in a bad mood, John. I'm just in a where-the-hell-am-I-going mood. I'm Sheila, but I guess you know that."

"Happy to make your acquaintances. I'm Christopher."

"Hello, Christopher."

"Yeah, hello Christopher. You remind me of someone. You look like my uncle."

"You talking about your Uncle Todd?"

"Yes, John. I am. He was the sweetest, kindest person in the world."

"I will take that as a compliment, young lady. Thank you."

"I could talk to Uncle Todd about anything. He would not only listen, he would understand. He would put his hands on my shoulders, look me right in the eyes, and tell me what I needed to do to solve my problem."

"Sheila, you're talking to Christopher as if you've known him for years."

"I guess I am. Christopher, are you my reincarnated Uncle Todd?"

"'Fraid not. But if I do say so, and I don't mean to beat my own chest, I'm like your uncle. If you want to talk to me about anything, I'm all ears. Sometimes it's good to talk to an uninvolved outsider who can be objective about things."

"Great. Here it goes. I fell in love with John a couple of years ago. He was this handsome, brilliant guy."

"I'm not handsome anymore, Sheila?"

"Hush. Let me talk. I need to get it out. So, I fell in love. We fell in love. The first year together was bliss. Then we moved in together. Then John lost his job and things started going downhill."

"They sure did. I don't think Sheila really understood or accepted the impact that had on our lives."

"Please, John. Let me talk. When he lost his job, it hurt him a lot. A little bit about the money and security, but mostly his pride. It was like a dagger in his heart. He started questioning himself, questioning our relationship. He became bitter, irascible, and sometimes weird with what he was thinking."

"I wasn't weird. I just had a lot on my mind. I know I didn't treat you very nicely, but I never stopped loving you."

"And I never stopped loving you. I tried to help you. I supported you. I gave you that unconditional love we talked about earlier. But you rejected me. You went off into your own little world."

"I didn't realize that. Sheila, I'm sorry. I'm sorry that you thought that I stopped loving you."

"It's good that you both stopped talking for the last minute. It tells me that you are digesting what Shelia just said, and what you, John, also said. You listened to each other's words, and now you're listening to yourself."

"You are like my uncle. In fact, you even smile like Uncle Todd used to."

"So, John and Sheila, here you are travelling

someplace in a physical sense, but not in a spiritual sense. You used to be kindred spirits, or as the kids now say, soulmates."

"Yeah, that's right. We were soulmates. Weren't we, Sheila?

"Pretty much. No...definitely. I miss that."

"So do I."

"Perhaps you should back-up."

"I don't think you're talking about your shoe, Christopher. Are you?"

"Yes, but that's secondary to you and Sheila backing up and looking hard at what you had. When I get my lost shoe, I'm going to clean the mud off it, and then shine them up. What are you going to do?"

⸻ ◆ ⸻

"Coopersville looks like a nice little town."

"Yeah. It does. If the college gives off the same vibe, I think I'm going to like it there."

"I'll tell you, John, this place feels good. I certainly want to continue with my blog. I really like doing it and it does bring in some money. But I've always wanted to open a shop, you know, a little store that sells whatever. The kind of place you see on TV shows where the owner gets to know everyone and becomes a real part of the town."

"I've not heard you talk that way before."

"What way?"

"For one thing, you're smiling. For another, your eyes are wide opened, like a little kid looking at the bicycle they just got for Christmas. I think *verve* is the best way to describe how you sound."

"All of that, John. All of that."

"There it is."

"Please don't tell me you're pointing at another shoe in the road."

"Sorry for laughing, but that's funny. No, no shoe. It's the bed and breakfast."

"The bed part sounds terrific. You did reserve a room with a fireplace and one king size bed, didn't you?"

"Sure did. Why that questioning look on your face?"

"He wasn't Uncle Todd reincarnated, was he?"

Shoulders

"Thank you, Christopher. Your observations and advice have been extremely helpful," said Ray Hagerty.

"You're most welcome," said Christopher. I was honored when management suggested I come here to help all of you. This is a great location and I'm sure you will all do very well. He bid farewell and left the meeting with the eight people who would oversee the remodeling of a small supermarket that went out of business. He stood outside the building before he walked to his hotel. He prayed, and knew that his prayers would definitely be heard. He made the sign of the cross and whispered, "Bless this place and bless all the people we will help."

Christopher had never been to the ocean, and very much looked forward to seeing it. He wanted to feel his feet digging into the sand; he wanted to hear the waves as they ended their journey and splashed down; he wanted to inhale salty air. He sat on a bench at the edge of the beach and removed his shoes and socks. He rolled-up his pants, sat up, stretched-out his arms, and said, "Here I go."

What a wonderful feeling, he thought, as his toes wiggled in the dry sand. He pushed down with one foot, lifted it, and said, "One step for man, one step for ..." The sound of someone crying interrupted him. Not far away he saw a young boy sitting on a park bench, his head down, crying. Christopher forgot about his walking on the sand, and went to help the boy. "What's the matter, son?"

The boy looked up at Christopher, wiped his tears with his hands, and said, "I'm not your son."

"You're right. But I don't know your name and old people like me tend to call young boys like you, son."

"Nothing."

Christopher sat down at the opposite end of the bench, and said, "I guess it was just the sand blowing up and getting into your eyes."

"My mom told me not to talk to strangers."

"Your mom is a very intelligent person for telling you that. Do you know why she told you that?"

The boy started to become engaged in the conversation. "Yeah, because some people are really bad and could do bad things."

"She is absolutely right. But remember that she said *some people*. That means that some people, probably most people, are good and want to do good things."

"So how do I know if you are a bad person or a good person?"

Christopher thought that was an intelligent question from such a young boy. "Well, we could just talk a little, and you can decide which one I am. My name is Christopher. What's your name?"

He looked up and down at Christopher and hesitated before he answered. "I guess telling you my name ain't going to hurt me. My name is Lucas."

Christopher smiled. He put his arm on the back of the bench to suggest companionship, but made sure it wasn't too close to Lucas. "How old are you, Lucas?"

"Ten."

"Whew. I'm a little older than that."

"How old?"

"Would you believe I'm almost two-hundred-years-old?"

Lucas burst out laughing. "You're not two-hundred. No one is."

Christopher sat back on the bench and extended his feet out. "I was about to take a walk on the sand. You don't have any shoes on, so how about keeping me company? By the way, Lucas, see those people over there?"

"Yeah. So?"

"We'll stay close to them as we walk, and if at any time you think I'm one of the *bads*, and not one of the *goods*, you can call out to them. Okay?"

"Okay."

Christopher returned to the bench where he left his shoes, and retrieved them. He was convinced that the good folks far outnumbered the bad folks, but he didn't want any of the bad folks to take his shoes. "Oh, did you want to leave your shoes over there?"

"They're not there."

Feigning a surprised look, Christopher asked, "Where are they?" Lucas pointed out and up. Christopher saw them – a pair of sneakers hanging from an electrical line that crossed the street. "Wow! How did you get up there to hang your sneakers?"

"I didn't." He then laughed, and said, "You're a very funny man."

"I hope you mean funny *ha ha*, not funny *peculiar*."

"Huh?"

"Not important. So, tell me, how did they get up there?"

They walked on the sand. Christopher was enjoying every moment of feeling the granules giving in to his weight, and finding rest between his toes. He listened attentively to everything Lucas was saying, while absorbing the spectacular view of an expansive blue-gray ocean meeting a bright blue sky. Lucas mostly looked down as he walked, occasionally picking up a sea shell or a nondescript item that he would inspect and then toss back onto the sand. "The guys threw them up there."

"Guys?"

"From my school. They thought it would be really funny. I shouldn't have left them on the bench when I came down here to look for shells."

"Boys will be boys."

"Yeah. But some boys are jerks. You know, they're…"

Christopher cleared his throat, interrupting him, and said, "I'm glad you didn't use a curse word. Jerks is a good word."

"Yeah, alright." Even though Christopher didn't ask any questions, Lucas kept on talking. He told him about his school, what he really likes and what he hates. "History. Yuk!" He told him about his mom. "I think I have the best mom in the world." He told him about his father. "He died before I was born."

Christopher knew about everything that Lucas told him, but it was good to hear Lucas talk about it. "I'm sorry you didn't have your dad with you while you were growing up, but you've become a very smart young man, with very good manners."

"Yeah, but Mom doesn't like to play catch with me, and she doesn't know anything about fixing a car, or how to fish."

"I see what you mean, Lucas." They sat crossed-legged in the sand to continue their discussion. The sun began to set. Christopher saw sunrises and sunsets before, but never from an ocean view. He was spellbound. "You okay, Mister?"

Christopher took-in a big breath, smiled, and said, "Yes, I am. I was just admiring the sunset. Lucas, do you know what the expression *a shoulder to lean on* means?"

"Yeah. Like you said. A shoulder to lean on. Like if I wanted to lean on something, I could do it on your shoulder."

"You are correct. But it really means a little more than that. It's someone that will listen to you if you have a problem or need some advice. It's someone that can help you, like help you feel better."

"You mean like my mom?"

"Yes. I also mean me. I like you, Lucas. I think you're a terrific kid." He reached into his breast pocket, pulled out a business card, and handed it to Lucas. "This is me. If you ever need a shoulder to lean on, you can call me."

"What is Goodwill?"

"It's a store that sells all sorts of stuff. People donate things they don't want anymore, like shoes or pants or shirts or even furniture. We sell those things, and with the money we make, we help people who need help. That's why I'm here. We're building a new Goodwill store about a half-mile from here."

The sun was about to completely set and not be seen again until the next morning. Christopher said, "Listen carefully and you might hear the sun saying *good night*."

Lucas gently tossed a sea shell at Christopher, and said, "You're pulling my leg."

"Speaking of legs, I have to get mine up. Have to go to my hotel and get a good night of sleep. I'm leaving very early tomorrow morning. Goodbye, Lucas. I really enjoyed meeting you"

"Goodbye." Shoeless Lucas walked back home.

———— ((•)) ————

The next morning the sun did rise. Over breakfast Lucas told his mom that he was going to try to get his sneakers down from the wire. "Let them be, Lucas. You have other sneakers. Hmm. What's that I see on your feet? Could they be sneakers? My oh my."

"But I like those other sneakers better. I'm going down to the beach. I want to collect more sea shells."

Lucas stood at the side of the road trying to invent a way to get the sneakers down. They were as high up as the roof on his house. He thought a giant ladder could reach them, but he didn't have a ladder – not a small one nor a giant one. He thought if he threw clam shells at them, they would somehow magically flip around and untie themselves from the wire. He leaned on the fire hydrant, looking up, when he heard a loud *honk*. A big trailer truck was slowly heading towards him. He moved a few feet away and the truck came to a stop at the side of the road very near him. He looked at the trailer, and back again at the sneakers. Three times. He ran to the cab and waved both hands enthusiastically. The driver rolled down his window, "What, kid?" By the tone of his voice, Lucas didn't think he was a very nice guy – not the kind of guy that would help a kid. But he was wrong. He explained his problem with his sneakers. "If I could get on top of your trailer, I could reach them. Please?"

"Sure, kid. Let me back-up a little so I'm under your sneakers." The truck backed-up very slowly. Lucas was well behind it. He wanted to be in charge of this exciting operation, and gave hand-signals to the driver, which the driver ignored, until he was directly under the sneakers. Lucas waved almost maniacally for the driver to stop. He put on his flashers and placed two orange traffic cones behind the trailer. "Ready? I'll give you a boost so you can get on top." Lucas put his foot on the driver's cupped hands and felt like he was flying up when the driver aggressively and quickly lifted him.

Lucas walked on top of the trailer and was directly under the sneakers. He reached-up and was frustrated that he couldn't reach them. He jumped up and his fingertips barely touched one of the sneakers. "Rrrrr!" he moaned.

The driver called up to him to see if he was okay. "Yeah, but I can't reach them."

"Sorry kid. At least we tried. Gotta get down now."

A passenger in the cab opened his door and called out, "Wait a minute." He went to the back of the trailer and climbed to the top. "Hey, kid. I have an idea. How about you sit on my shoulders?"

"Are you a shoulder to lean on?"

"Well, kind of, I guess." The guy hoisted Lucas up. "Now listen very carefully. Do not, I repeat, do *not* touch the wire. Only touch the sneakers. Got it?"

Lucas said, "Got it."

"Repeat what I just said." Lucas did, and by doing

so, he was able to untangle them, get them down, and not be electrocuted.

"Got 'em! I got 'em." He got off the man's shoulders and thanked him.

"Happy to help, son. If you ever need some shoulders to sit on, I'm your guy." Lucas was about to say *I'm not your son*, but thought better of it. Acting like a grown-up, he shook the man's hand, and smiled. Both of them climbed off the trailer. Lucas ran home to tell his mom what happened. He was more excited at that moment than he could ever remember.

"No sneakers in church, young man."

Lucas ran back up the stairs and put on shoes. He took three steps at a time coming down the steps. There was a knock at the door. Lucas's mom went to the door, and without opening it, said, "Yes, can I help you?"

A man replied, "Yes, I think you can."

There was something about his voice, something familiar. Uncharacteristically, she opened the door without knowing who it was. When she saw the man, she stepped back, put her hand on her heart, and said, "You?"

"Yes, me."

"Who is it, Mom?"

"It's...ahh, it's an old friend." Lucas came to the door, and said, "You?"

The man replied, "You?"

Lucas's mom was frozen. She was not only

confused by you-you questions, she also found herself in emotional turmoil.

"I want to talk to you, Liz. I *need* to talk to you."

She told Lucas to please go up to his bedroom. "I need to talk to this man, alone. Now go."

She stepped further back, and the man entered the house. He pulled out a folded piece of paper from his pocket, and unfolded it. "I didn't know how to say this, and I didn't want to screw-up what I have to tell you, so I wrote it down."

He looked at the paper, his eyes glancing from left to right while he read what he wrote, but he didn't speak. He started to cry. His lips were quivering. He crumpled the paper, looked lovingly at Liz, and said, "I am no one without you. I need you in my life. What I did to you cannot be forgiven, but I beg you to forgive me."

"What happened, Owen? You were here one day and gone the next. I thought you died. My heart was broken. I grieved for you for more time than I can remember. All I wanted in life was you, especially after Lucas was born. Sure, I had the money you left in the bank account, and I get a check every month from that trust you set-up. The money helped me stay alive, me and Lucas. But I wasn't alive. Not for a long, long time. Now you step into my house, the house we used to live in together, and you ask me to forgive you?" Liz also started to cry, and her tears quickly turned into anger. She erupted and nearly screamed, "How dare you! How dare you!"

Owen wanted to hug her, hold her and comfort her, but he knew that would be an unwelcomed gesture. He gave her a moment to shed her tears, and then told her what happened. Stammering and trying to hold back his tears, he said, "I was an addict. Heroin mostly. Hidden from you. I was what people called a *controlled user.* When you told me that you were pregnant the controlled part went away. Maybe the timing was coincidental, or maybe the thought of being a father scared the crap out of me. I don't know. But I quickly started using more. I knew I was a junkie, and I didn't want you to know. Junkies live in chaos. Nothing made sense to me. For a few years I lived on the streets. I became a beggar and a thief to survive."

"Why didn't you tell me? Why didn't you come to me and ask for help?"

"Chaos clouded my mind. I often thought about suicide, but I needed a fix to work up the courage. And when I got the fix, I forgot about suicide"

"Are you still a junkie?"

"No, absolutely not. I committed a crime – a theft – and got sent to prison for five years. It was the best thing that could have happened to me."

"Prison was the best thing?"

"Yes. I went through rehab. My addiction stopped. I had lots of sessions with a shrink and a social worker. Last year I felt whole again. Me again. I was clean. I had my head on right. So many times, I wanted to call you or write to you. But I didn't want to risk it. I didn't want your life to be ruined by an ex-junkie convict showing up at your doorstep."

"But here you are."

She looked at him with perplexed anger.

"Here I am." He folded his hands on his lap, leaned forward, and looked at her with pleading eyes. She heard his words, his confession, and saw his face looking at her, asking for forgiveness. She started to realize that she never stopped loving him. She wanted to say *come home*, but the hurt she felt wouldn't allow it.

Lucas came into the room. "Lucas, I have to talk to you about something."

"No, you don't, Mom. I was on the steps. I heard everything." He walked over to Owen. They looked at each other for almost a minute without saying a word. Lucas put his hands on Owen's shoulders, and said, "Should I call you Owen, or Dad?"

Roberto joined Renyard Accident Law Group by accident. It was not the first accident that would affect his life. He was an undergraduate seeking a degree in political science. In his second year he suffered a broken arm due to the negligence of an Uber driver. His friend recommended that he talk with Renyard about suing the driver. He did.

"Hi, I'm here to see Mr. Galworth. I'm Roberto Alvarado"

"I bet it's about your arm," said the receptionist. Roberto smiled, and said, "Is my cast and sling that visible?" She laughed, and buzzed Galworth. A moment later he was greeted, and escorted into a small conference room. They talked for thirty minutes. Five minutes was spent on Roberto's accident; 25 minutes was spent in a Q&A session while Galworth got to know him. Roberto was unaware that he was being interviewed. Galworth liked what he was hearing from the well-mannered, intelligent man, and offered him a job. Roberto would be a part-time clerk, which synced with his college schedule, and he accepted the position with gratitude.

As time went by, Roberto found the work and the discipline it took to be a lawyer, was far more interesting and stimulating than poly sci. With the encouragement of Galworth and other attorneys at the firm, as well as the firm's financial support, Roberto dropped out of college and started law school. During his three years in law school, Roberto was an apprentice at Reynard, studying law, and also seeing it in action. Law was becoming part of his DNA. He spent his waking hours at work, at law school, and at home studying. Socializing became a low priority. Although he had a casual date now and then, he was more interested in his job than his companion, much to the dissatisfaction of his date. His friends told him that he shouldn't waste away his years of being a *stud.* His best friend told him, "If you don't balance your life with a career *and* a woman, you'll become a brilliant lawyer, but a lonely man." Roberto paid only lip service to his friend's advice.

Galworth called him into his office the day after he graduated from law school. "I have three very important things to discuss." His face looked stern. He cleared his throat, and said, "First, we helped you with law school. I need to remind you of your contractual commitment to work here."

Roberto drew a check mark in the air, and said, "Check. Guaranteed."

"Good. Second, I was told that you graduated with honors. When that happens, there's a little thing we do for our staff." The door opened and all of the staff marched in, applauding Roberto and congratulating him. Cake was served after Roberto blew out the one candle which was in the image of Lady Justice. The party broke-up and Galworth told Roberto to have a seat.

Roberto made another air-checkmark, nodded, and thanked Galworth.

"Okay, we got one and two out of the way. Now here's number three, perhaps the most important thing." Roberto's mind raced through several possibilities of what Galworth was about to tell him, but he was wrong on every one of them. "You need shiny shoes, Roberto. You're giving our clients the wrong image with those...what are they? Loafers?"

Roberto made his third checkmark. "New job, new shoes. Got it!" Galworth reached out to Roberto and shook his hand. Uncharacteristically, he gave him a hug. Roberto was on cloud nine.

———⚫———

Lin Takata was a dedicated nurse with a heart of gold. If the hospital's patients voted on who was the best nurse there, Lin would win the trophy, hands down.

After three years as an RN, and being intrigued by all things medical, she decided to go back to school part-time, and become a nurse practitioner. She told her roommate, Leeann, "I know working full time and school part-time is a grind, but I really want to do that."

Leeann let out a "Ha!" and said, "Darlin' I think you should go all the way. Brain surgeon!"

Pretending to be serious, Lin said, "Hmm, not a bad idea. And then I'll marry a rocket scientist."

"Great idea. Here we go." They sat back and started to view the 1948 movie, "The Red Shoes." While the introductory credits were scrolling, Leeann said, "Pay attention, darlin'. This story is really about you."

"How so?"

"The star is a ballerina. She's torn between her

dedication to her career as a dancer, and her desire to be with a man she loves."

"So?"

"If she was a nurse instead of a ballerina, she'd be playing your life story. You need to have a man in your life."

"Yeah. Later. After I become a brain surgeon."

In the morning, Lin and Leeann walked to the grocery store. There was an empty trashcan that apparently rolled into the street. Lin was concerned that a car would hit it, so she went to retrieve it. But it was too late. A car hit the trashcan which shot like a cannon ball and hit the front wheel of a bike messenger's bike. The messenger lost control and was heading toward a woman wheeling her baby carriage. The woman screamed and pushed the carriage out of the way. It unfortunately ran into a woman carrying two grocery bags. One of the bags flipped into the air and hit Leeann. She was knocked off her feet and took a bad fall. She was bruised and held her leg as she cried out in pain.

Lin's triage training kicked-in. She pointed to the bike messenger and told him to call 911. "Now!" She kneeled down next to Leeann and quickly determined that the bruises were not remarkable, but her leg was. "Don't move. An ambulance will be here soon. Breath. Stay as relaxed as you can." Next in order was the baby in the carriage. "She's fine," she told the mother. She then checked the woman who was hit by the baby carriage, then the man in the car, and lastly, the bike messenger. Only Leeann was hurt in the bizarre accident. The ambulance arrived and Leeann was taken to the hospital where Lin worked.

Leeann spent the night in the hospital. Morning came and Lin visited her. "Good morning, my most wonderful patient. The cast looks good on you."

"Yeah, it's the new Vera Wang model."

"My shift ends in a couple of hours. I have an appointment with a lawyer about your accident. It's the Renyard law firm.

"That was quick."

"Time waits for no man. No woman, that it is. See ya before I leave. Kissy kissy."

"Hi, I'm Lin Takata. I have an appointment with…"

"With one of our best lawyers, Norman Olson. Please have a seat and I'll let him know you're here."

Moments later, Olson greeted Lin. "Please come into my office."

He got all the specifics about the accident that he needed, and told her that he would be getting a copy of the incident report from the police, and will follow-up. "It was a pleasure meeting you, Ms. Takata." Just before Lin turned to walk out the door, Roberto walked by reading a document. He didn't look up to see Lin exiting, and Lin only saw the back of his head as he passed by.

Lin decided to have an afternoon latte at Starbucks, located just down the block from Renyard's. While waiting for her drink to be made, two customers were chatting about their new shoes. "Love 'em. Love yours too. 70% off! Cool beans!"

Lin had a flashback of the movie she watched last night. She looked down at her black, well-worn Clarks and gave thought to getting a new pair. "Excuse me gals. I couldn't help hearing you talking about your shoes. They're beautiful. Where did you buy them?"

"Shoe Magic around the corner is going out of business."

"Thanks. Just might go there."

"Today's their last day, so you might want to go pretty soon."

"Thanks, again."

⸺ ⊙ ⸻

Christopher thanked Bruce Milner, the owner/manager of Shoe Magic. "Goodwill will pick-up the shoes tomorrow morning," said Christopher.

Milner said, "On one hand, I hope I don't have many to donate. I really would like to recoup some of the money I spent on buying them. On the other hand, if I do have any unsold merchandise, I'm glad it's going for a good cause.

The deal that Christopher and Milner struck involved any inventory that Shoe Magic didn't sell. As Bruce told him, he purchased almost all of his footwear from a supplier that just went out of business and they could not accept any returns.

When Christopher walked out of his backroom office, he saw as many shoppers as there were pairs of shoes. It was a mob scene of people grabbing and opening boxes, and trying on the footwear. He finally made his way to the front of the store where there were two lines of people checking-out. It was havoc at the cash register. He glanced at the people in line who seemed happy that they bought new shoes for a very low price. He disregarded that he was being jostled, and felt happy that they were happy.

"Thank you. Next!" said the cashier as Lin walked away with her new red Clarks. The adjacent cashier said the same thing to Roberto, as he walked away with his new shiny dress shoes. They bumped into each other when they tried to avoid the throngs of people, and both said "Sorry," but neither looked at the other.

━━━━━━◄(O)►━━━━━━

Seeing that Leeann was awake, Lin walked into her room with a cheerful smile. "Goooood morning!"

"Is it?"

"Yeah, it is. Seems you have a proximal tibia incomplete fracture."

"Thank you, Nurse Nightingale. English?"

"You cracked your shin bone. It will take a while to heal, and you'll have to stay off your feet."

"Yeah, the doc said I couldn't play soccer for a while. I told him I didn't play soccer, and he said, 'no problem then.'"

"Very funny. You'll be released later today after they take one more x-ray."

"Yippity do dah!"

With a serious tone, Lin asked, "Speaking of walking around, do you wear size eleven men's shoes?"

"When I get home, I'll check my shoe rack."

Lin told her that she bought a new pair of shoes, but the packages must have gotten mixed-up when she paid for them. "Some guy out there is going to be prancing around in red Clarks."

"So return them."

"Can't. Yesterday was the last day they were open."

"So the *Going Out of Business* sign really meant they were going out of business?"

"Yup. I could put them on eBay, but I got them cheap, so even if I throw them away, I haven't lost much."

"Donate them, Lin. You'll feel good about doing that."

―――――∞«◊»∞―――――

"Good morning, Mr. Graduate," said Galworth when Roberto arrived at Renyard's. "I'd rather call you *Mr. Shiny Shoes*, but that would be a misnomer."

Roberto explained what happened at Shoe Magic, and showed him the red Clarks. Galworth was gracious in accepting the explanation, and strongly suggested to Roberto to "Go buy new shoes!"

Roberto walked around the office and asked each of the 20 female staffers if they wore a size 6 shoe. Three women wore a size 6, but none wanted red shoes. One woman told him he should give them to Goodwill.

―――――∞«◊»∞―――――

"Hello. Donating today?" asked Christopher.

"Yes. Just a pair of shoes."

"They look brand new. Are they?"

"Yes. Thanks. Have a good day."

Lin got in her car and started her engine.

Christopher noticed a car pulling up towards the donation entrance. He signaled Lin to lower her window. "I forgot something, could you just wait a tiny moment. I'll be right back." He placed the Shoe Magic shoe box on a shelf.

Roberto stopped his car in back of Lin's, got out, and walked towards Christopher. "Good morning, sir. Donation?"

Roberto handed Christopher the shoe box, and said, "Yes, here you go."

He was startled when he heard Lin scream out, "Wait!" She got out of her car, took the shoe box she just donated off the shelf that Christopher had placed it on, and said, "Want to trade?"

"Unbelievable!" said Roberto. "What are the chances?"

Christopher said, "Yes, what *are* the chances?"

Roberto and Lin chit-chatted for a few moments about the coincidence of shopping at the same time, and donating at the same time. She liked his face. He looked like a young Antonio Banderas – handsome, black hair, brown eyes.

He had recently watched *Kill Bill Volume II,* and the image of Lucy Liu popped into his head as he looked at her.

They shook hands, but didn't shake. They just stared at each other for a few seconds. He liked the feel of her delicate, but strong hand; she liked the feel of his masculine, yet gentle grip.

"Goodbye."
"Goodbye."
They departed in their cars.

———◦((◦))◦———

A month later, Lin and Leeann visited Renyard's for an up-date on Leeann's lawsuit. In the glass enclosed conference room, Norman Olson told Leeann things are looking very good. He recounted what her insurance company, and the insurance companies of the other four people involved in the accident said. "It's complicated, but we're working it out. Looks like you'll have zero out-of-pocket cost for the ambulance, hospital, and therapy sessions."

"That's a relief," said Leeann. "How about that thing you call *punishment damages*?"

"You mean punitive damages. We're working on it and we *will* solve the puzzle. Right now, everyone's pointing a finger at someone else, but their finger will also be pointing at themselves."

Olson then told them that he went a step further. "The police report didn't have any mention of whose garbage pail caused all of this. The owner is definitely part of the nexus. We found out who it is, and we're going to be following-up with him." While Olson talked, Roberto was walking down the hallway. His eye caught the red shoes that Lin was wearing. He had to find out if it was her.

Knock, knock. "Sorry for interrupting." Lin turned around and saw Roberto; he saw her. Their eyes locked. He stood still while looking at her. There was an excitement running through him that he couldn't explain. Lin sat still. She also had a visceral reaction to seeing him.

Leeann fanned her face with her hand, and said, "Whew! Getting warm in here."

"This sounds very forward, and I apologize. But Ms. Red Shoes, when you're finished with Norm, can I buy you a cup of coffee?"

Leeann whispered, "Not warm. Hot."

Lin blushed, stood up, extended her hand to Roberto, and said, "Yes, I would like that."

"**A**dios, Rich. Hope to see ya tomorrow night, but I really don't hope that I see ya tomorrow night." Vickey Sandler was speaking to the door that was left open when her husband left the house. She was an unhappy, bitter, 26-year-old wife and mother. Her husband was a plumber who worked hard on weekdays, and drank hard on weekends. Her daughter, Priscilla, soon to be 10-years-old, bore the brunt of her mother's unhappiness.

"And where are you going at this hour of the night, young lady?"

"In the backyard. I want to look at the stars."

Vickey put her hands on her hips, looked sternly at Priscilla, and said, "The dishes before the stars." She went to the family room, sat down on the sofa, and clicked on the TV. Scrolling through the guide, she decided to watch *The Wizard of Oz.*

Priscilla glanced at the TV as she proceeded to the kitchen to clean-up the dinner dishes, pots, and pans. "Mom, could you please put it on pause till I finish in here?"

"I'm going to sleep early tonight, so, no. Work fast and you won't miss much."

Priscilla did work fast, but also very carefully. She knew that if she missed cleaning a spot on a dish, or heaven forbid, dropped and broke a plate, the evening would be spent listening to her mother chastising her. When she joined her mother to watch the movie, her eyes were glued to the TV. She had seen the movie before, but this time she was absorbed in the storyline.

Vickey said, "This is the umpteenth time I saw this movie. I don't know why I'm watchin' it again."

"Maybe because it's a good movie."

"I used to think your father was the Wizard of Oz. Now, I'm not sure if he's the one without a heart or the one without a brain."

Priscilla didn't respond to her mother's denigrating comments about her father. If she did, an argument would ensue and she'd wind up in her bedroom, and not be able to watch the movie. She clenched her teeth, and as she often does to calm herself, slowly counted to ten while slowly breathing in and out.

Before the movie ended, Vickey was fast asleep on the sofa. Priscilla lowered the sound, hoping that her mother would not wake until the end of the movie. When the movie was ending, Dorothy's line, *"There's no place like home,"* hit home for Priscilla. She mumbled inaudibly, *I hope there is another place*, and her eyes began to tear.

Priscilla turned the TV off and awakened her mother. Vickey grunted and marched herself up the steps to her bedroom. There was no hug, no kiss, no *sweet dreams.* All Vickey said was, "Turn the lights off before you go to bed."

Priscilla turned the lights off and went to the backyard. She gazed at the stars that seemed to twinkle, seeming to be sending her a signal. *Is that where Oz is, somewhere over the rainbow,* she thought. *Can I get there?*

⸺◉⸺

"Good morning, my wonderful students!" said Ms. Wembly, the fifth-grade teacher at Priscilla's school. "Thanksgiving is in two weeks, so I thought it would be fun, and educational, to talk about that holiday." She introduced Christopher, who volunteered to make the rounds at many grade schools, to talk about the history of the holiday, and, more importantly, its meaning.

Christopher thanked Ms. Wembly for the introduction, and walked to the front of the classroom. Some children smiled when they saw him, some laughed. "I do look funny, don't I?" he said.

"First, let me tell you how I am dressed." He spent a couple of minutes talking about his cotton shirt, his doublet, slops, monmouth cap, and latchet shoes. "They made all of their own clothing. There were no stores like Goodwill, which is where I work, to walk around racks and racks of shirts and pants and dresses."

Christopher lectured the students on the history of the pilgrims, their two-month voyage across the Atlantic, and the many hardships they faced during their journey and after they arrived in America. "I'm sure you met many very nice people in your life. People who are happy to help you if you need help. Well, the Pilgrims met some very nice people. *Indians!*"

A girl in the back of the classroom raised her hand, and when recognized by Christopher, said, "Did the Indians cook the turkey for them? I don't like turkey." Another kid called out, "Cranberries. Yuk!" Another screamed, "Pumpkin pie," and then pretended to regurgitate. Within seconds nearly all of the kids were crying out about the foods they didn't like, and the foods they did like. "We should serve hamburgers on Thanksgiving," said one kid. The cacophony was disturbing to Ms. Wembly who wanted to hush her students. Christopher whispered to her to allow them to speak out. "It's good to speak out about what you like and don't like. And they're kids. They'll stop soon." He did notice one girl who did not join the other kids in their raucous soundings, and made a mental note of her.

The students did calm down. "Whew. I'll now answer your question young lady. No, the Indians didn't cook a turkey for the Pilgrims. But they did teach the Pilgrims how to plant seeds and grow food, like corn, beans, and squash. They taught them how to be farmers. And the Pilgrims were very thankful for that."

"Did they teach them how to hunt?" asked one of the students.

"Yes, they did."

Another asked, "What else did they teach them?"

Christopher raised his arms, and with great enthusiasm said, "You are very smart to ask that question. By helping the Pilgrims, by caring about them, the Pilgrims realized how important home and family are. And that's what we should all be thankful for."

Priscilla tensed when she heard 'home and family.' She raised her hand. "Yes, Priscilla? asked Ms. Wembly.

"Can I be excused?"

"Yes, but don't be long." Priscilla left the room, ostensibly to visit the girls' room, but decided to just walk the halls, banging the side of her fist on the lockers as she walked. She added to the clanking sound by muttering *bang* with each jab. After a hundred steps or so, she stopped, and counted to ten as she took big breaths in and out. When she returned to the classroom, Christopher had already departed.

⸺◆⸺

During lunch in the school cafeteria the next day, Priscilla noticed a man a few tables away talking with a teacher. She thought it might have been that pilgrim guy, but wasn't sure. When the teacher left, Christopher waved to Priscilla. Having finished her lunch, she went over to him. "You're that pilgrim, aren't you?"

"I was yesterday, but today I'm just Christopher." He gestured to her to take a seat next him, and said, "Please join me."

A man dressed as an American Indian was walking around the lunch room handing out free ice cream bars. "Let's have one," said Christopher. Priscilla nodded yes.

"Here you go, young lady. And one for you, sir."

"Thank you," said Christopher.

"Yes, thank you," said Priscilla.

"Happy Thanksgiving to both of you."

Christopher and Priscilla started to eat their ice cream bars. "So, what did you think about my story about the pilgrims and Thanksgiving?" he asked.

"It was okay. I mean, I knew a lot about that, but I guess I didn't know that the Indians taught them about farming."

Christopher continued to ease into what he knew upset Priscilla. "I think holidays are very important. All of them. What's your favorite holiday?"

She let out a *Ha,* and said, "The ones when school is closed." Christopher laughed.

"My favorites are the ones that remind us to say something or do something. Especially something nice."

She looked at him with a quizzical expression, and said, "Like what?"

"I like Christmas the most."

"Yeah, that's a good holiday. *No school!* Do you believe in Santa Claus?"

Christopher squinted, and said, "Hmm. Well, when I was your age, I wanted to believe there was a Santa. I knew if I was nice, I would get a gift."

"Yeah, like that song, *'If you're naughty or nice.'*"

"Yup, that one. And I also like Valentine's Day because it reminds everyone to tell someone that they are loved. And I like Mother's Day and Father's Day because it's also a reminder to say thank you and I love you. Thanksgiving..."

Priscilla interrupted him, and said, "I don't like Thanksgiving."

"Hmm. Why not?"

"Because I don't like to lie."

He knew exactly what she meant, but knew it was important for her to speak about it before he gave her his point-of-view...his advice. "Why would you have to lie on Thanksgiving?"

"You said that the pilgrims were thankful for their home and for their family. I'm not. I'd rather be in Kansas or Oz."

He was fully aware of why she said that, but *telling* her would be far less effective than her telling it herself. "Oz, what a fantastic place. I know the movie. It's wonderful." He waited for her to say more, but she remained silent as her tongue swirled around the mound of chocolate chip ice cream. "What do you think was the best part of *The Wizard of Oz?*" he asked.

"When they got what they needed. You know, the heart and brain and courage. And when Dorothy got what she wanted. That's what I want. I want red shoes so I can go wherever I want to go."

Christopher was pleased that Priscilla was opening up about what she wanted, and it was clear that she wanted to escape from an unhappy home life. "I liked the good witch Glinda."

"Why?"

Christopher finished his ice cream, and wiped his mouth with a napkin. He smiled at Priscilla, and said, "I really enjoyed that." He placed the stick from the ice cream bar on his napkin, cleared his throat, and leaned forward to have a closer emotional connection with her. "Well, Glinda just wanted to do good things for people, for Dorothy. But she knew that it was better for Dorothy to figure out what her heart needed. You know, to figure out how to solve her problems and be with people that loved her, and that she loved."

"Yeah, I know. That's what that song is all about, isn't it? You know, that *somewhere over the rainbow* song."

Christopher put his hand on her hand. He looked at her with gentle, caring eyes, and said, "Yes and no. The song is about her wanting to find another place, a place where she and Toto would be safe." He watched Priscilla absorbing his words.

"You know, Dorothy thought that nobody wanted to help her. She didn't realize that all of them had jobs to do and they couldn't take the time right then and there to help her."

"But they didn't help her."

"No, not at that time. But if Dorothy waited until they weren't so busy, they probably would listen to her. And because they loved her, they would help her."

Priscilla kept licking her ice cream. Christopher could tell that she was thinking about his words. He asked, "Do you remember what Glinda said to her?"

"Kinda. Didn't she say to click her heels and she would be able to go wherever she wanted?"

Christopher replied in kind. "Kinda. But there was another thing that Glinda said. Do you remember what she said about home?"

"There's no place like home. Right?"

Christopher was delighted with her answer. "You're exactly right. Now there's another thing Glinda said to Dorothy about a backyard. Do you remember what it was?"

Priscilla frowned, trying to remember what Glinda said. She offered, "You can be happy in your backyard, at home."

"Three in a row, Priscilla. You have a great memory." He cleared his throat and said, "So what do you think Glinda meant by that?"

"I don't know. Go home? Or maybe you should go home and be with your family? Or, your family will not let that bad woman hurt Toto?"

Christopher raised his hands in the air, leaned back on his chair, and said in a very happy voice, "Ta dah! You are absolutely, positively, very, very, right!"

Priscilla couldn't stop smiling for being right, and for being complimented. "So Dorothy went back to Kansas and talked to her family and friends about her problem. And, of course, they listened. And, of course, they helped her."

"What about Dorothy's shoes?"

"Oh, the ruby slippers. That was...how do I say this?...a fun thing to put in the movie so people would think the slippers had a magical power."

"They didn't, though, did they?"

Christopher reached down to the package he had placed under the table, and handed it to Priscilla. "This is for you. You can use this to remind yourself about Dorothy's problem with the bad lady with the cat, and about home, and about people who love you." He stood up, extended his hand to Priscilla, and said, "I have to get back to work now. It was a pleasure talking with you. Bye, bye."

Priscilla also stood up, and held his hand for longer than a quick handshake. "Thank you for the ice cream. And oh, thank you for telling me about the movie. And, ah, thank you for whatever is in this box." She giggled, and said, "Bye."

Priscilla opened the gift she received. It was a pair of ruby slippers. She looked at them for a long time, and during all of that time she thought about her problem with her parents. She finally rose from her chair, and called out into the air, "There's no place like home."

Saturday rolled around the next day. Vickey was very surprised when she entered her kitchen to find Priscilla there, and seeing two cups ready for the hot coffee Priscilla just made. "What do we have here?" asked Vickey.

"I never made coffee for you, so now that I'm growing up, I thought I should." She poured some coffee into her mother's cup. "There's milk and sugar. Oops. I forgot the spoon." She retrieved a couple of spoons from the cupboard and placed them on the table.

"You're going to have coffee too?"

"No, that cup's for dad."

Vickey was beside herself. She was certainly not accustomed to seeing her daughter act the way she was acting, and was startled by what Priscilla was saying. "Yo, good morning," said Rich when he came into the kitchen. He didn't know that Priscilla had made the coffee, but when Vickey told him, all he could say was, "Wow!"

Priscilla got her large glass of orange juice and joined them at the table. "I don't remember everything when I was growing up, like when I was two or five. I do remember that both of you took care of me. I remember going to the playground, and the zoo, and the park, and the merry-go-round."

Vickey and Rich had no idea why Priscilla said that, and were somewhat shocked by hearing their little girl speak that way.

"Something happened. I don't know what. I know that you, Mom, were 16-years-old when I was born. And you, Dad, were 18. I think you had me because you were in love." Priscilla paused, purposely letting her words sink-in. In a matter-of-fact way, she said, "Why aren't you now?"

Her parents were frozen, holding their cups of coffee off the table, but not drinking. They were shocked by what she said. The silence was awkward. Neither one was able to answer. Priscilla waited, without saying a word. She remained motionless and just looked at her parents. Her mother put down her coffee cup and looked at her husband. "I don't know what happened to us. Do you?"

He put down his cup and lowered his head, and spoke to his lap. "Neither do I, but I think it just happened. You know, it happens to lots of people the longer they're together."

"Yes, I guess it does. But I don't like it. I don't like that you work so hard and come home late. And I hate that you disappear on Saturday nights to get drunk with your friends." She started to cry.

He raised his head and turned to her. "I work hard to make enough money for all of us. And I drink with my friends because I have fun with them."

Still crying, Vickey said, "We used to have fun together. Why can't we still have fun? I can do more. I can get a part-time job so you don't have to work so hard."

Rich held back his tears. He always wanted to think of himself as a macho man, and macho men don't cry. "I've been an ass, haven't I? Sorry, Pris, that's not good language."

"It's okay, Dad. I heard worse at school, and I could teach you some new words." All of them started laughing.

Rich took a sip of coffee while he thought about what to say to Vickey. "I thought you didn't want to... you... ah...decided to watch TV a lot." Vickey understood exactly what he was suggesting, and as they would find out in later years, so did Priscilla.

"I thought you lost interest, and I needed to take my mind off it. TV took my mind off it." said Vickey.

The conversation stopped, but the communication didn't. Vickey put her hand on his shoulder; he put his hand on top of hers. They looked at each other for a few seconds. Words were not needed. Their eyes communicated how they felt.

Vickey was thrilled with what her mom and dad were saying, and how they were looking at each other. "Dad, you used to kiss Mom in the morning. It's morning."

Vickey said, "Out of the mouths of babes." They kissed.

The day rolled on. At lunchtime, Rich said, "Hey, anyone want to try that new taco place that opened?"

"I'm game," said Vickey.

"If game means yes, I'm game too," said Priscilla..

Their afternoon was spent walking around the neighborhood park, playing frisbee, and talking – talking more than they had for several years.

Rich barbecued hamburgers while Vickey and Priscilla prepared a simple salad and cooked corn-on-the-cob. Vickey told her mom, "Did you know we're eating corn because Indians taught us how to grow it?"

Vickey smiled, and said, "Yes, I do. But I'm thankful that I can just buy it at the supermarket." Both of them laughed.

With dinner finished, and clean-up accomplished, Priscilla kissed her mom and dad on their cheeks, and said, "I'm tired. Goin' to bed. Night." Soon after she was in bed, and just before she dozed off, she heard her mom and dad giggling as they walked up the steps to their bedroom. The last sound Priscila heard was their bedroom door closing. She looked down from her bed at the ruby slippers on the floor, and said, "There's no place like home."

About the Author

About the Author

Jim Surmanek was born in Brooklyn, New York, in 1941, an otherwise good year, save the attack on Pearl Harbor. In his senior year of an undistinguished passage through Flushing High School, he accepted the prestigious position of part-time mailroom clerk at Parade magazine. Being skillful at sorting mail, the research director at Parade offered him his second prestigious position, research assistant, a job requiring that he endlessly crunch statistics. A significant turning point in his till then non-illustrious career happened when the Ogilvy & Mather advertising agency, apparently desperate for help, hired him as media research supervisor. He climbed the corporate ladder with only an occasional misstep at O&M, then J. Walter Thompson, and later at McCann-Erickson. He collected various business cards while he worked in the advertising business, all with his name and titles like executive media director, senior vice president, and general manager. The cards also had various addresses, which included New York City, Chicago, Los Angeles, and Mexico City. The only card he now has is personal, listing his name and address in Arizona. Writing, painting, carpentry, creating crafts, playing pickleball, and playing golf, in addition to connecting with his family and friends, have filled his days.